"It's very nice of you to offer me a place to stay." Savannah regarded him warily.

"But," she continued, "I'm sure that when your sister offered you a place to stay, she wasn't expecting you to pass it on to a random stranger."

Savannah wasn't a stranger. Carter had carried her photograph around in his pocket for two months.

For a moment it looked as if Savannah was wavering. But then her chin came up.

"You don't have to worry about me. I know you were Rob's friend, but I'm not your responsibility."

"When I make a promise, I keep it."

"And you did. You delivered Rob's message—"

"Not that promise," Carter interrupted. "I'm a marine, ma'am. And we never leave a man—or a woman—behind."

* * *

Texas Twins: Two sets of twins,
torn apart by family secrets, find their way home.

Her Surprise Sister—Marta Perry
July 2012

Mirror Image Bride—Barbara McMahon
August 2012

Carbon Copy Cowboy—Arlene James
September 2012

Look-Alike Lawman—Glynna Kaye
October 2012

The Soldier's Newfound Family—Kathryn Springer
November 2012

Reunited for the Holidays—Jillian Hart
December 2012

Books by Kathryn Springer

Love Inspired

Tested by Fire
Her Christmas Wish
By Her Side
For Her Son's Love
A Treasure Worth Keeping
Hidden Treasures
Family Treasures
Jingle Bell Babies
**A Place to Call Home*
**Love Finds a Home*
**The Prodigal Comes Home*
The Prodigal's Christmas Reunion
**Longing for Home*
**The Promise of Home*
The Soldier's Newfound Family

*Mirror Lake

Love Inspired Single Title

Front Porch Princess
Hearts Evergreen
"A Match Made for Christmas"
Picket Fence Promises
The Prince Charming List

KATHRYN SPRINGER

is a lifelong Wisconsin resident. Growing up in a "newspaper" family, she spent long hours as a child plunking out stories on her mother's typewriter and hasn't stopped writing since! She loves to write inspirational romance because it allows her to combine her faith in God with her love of a happy ending.

The Soldier's Newfound Family

Kathryn Springer

Special thanks and acknowledgment
to Kathryn Springer for her contribution
to the Texas Twins miniseries.

™ LOVE INSPIRED BOOKS

ISBN-13: 978-0-373-81655-2

THE SOLDIER'S NEWFOUND FAMILY

This edition published by arrangement with Love Inspired Books.

www.LoveInspiredBooks.com

Printed in U.S.A.

We ought always to thank God for you, brothers,
and rightly so, because your faith is
growing more and more, and the love
every one of you has for each other is increasing.

—*2 Thessalonians* 1:3

This book is warmly dedicated to my continuity cohorts—Marty, Barbara, Arlene, Glynna and Jill.

For wisdom, grace, patience and a sense of humor while we linked the Texas Twins books together.

It was a blessing working with you!

Chapter One

"And this one's Asteroid Man..."

Another plastic action figure landed on Sergeant Carter Wallace's lap tray, adding to the growing number of soldiers that had formed a perimeter around the coffee cup the flight attendant had set down in front of him.

"I got him for my birthday." A pair of eyes the color of Texas bluebonnets regarded Carter solemnly, waiting for his opinion.

"Cool." Just like the coffee he hadn't taken a sip of yet.

A wide, gap-toothed grin rearranged the pattern of butterscotch freckles on the preschool boy's cheeks. "He can fly, too. And the bad guys can't see him coming because he's *inbisible* when he lands."

Across the narrow aisle, the boy's harassed grandmother caught Carter's eye and mouthed the words *I'm sorry* as she tried to calm the fussy toddler in her lap.

The frustrated looks the woman had been receiving from their fellow passengers had only compounded her stress. Which explained why she hadn't noticed her grandson unbuckle his seat belt and commandeer the empty seat beside Carter after the beverage cart rattled past.

Without an invitation, the kid had settled in next to him and announced that his name was Josh and that he was four years old.

"Are you a real soldier?" he'd whispered, staring at the patches on Carter's camo jacket in open fascination.

Carter wrestled back a smile. "Yes, I am."

"I like soldiers."

Those three simple words had derailed Carter's plan to get some shut-eye. Josh had plunged both hands into a backpack and proceeded to pull out his action figures, an eclectic blend of superheroes and guys in camouflage, all working together to save the world.

The kid might have prevented Carter from the luxury of a long-overdue nap, but he'd also kept the nightmares at bay.

At least for a few hours.

"This is Mike." Josh carefully placed another action figure behind a Lego bunker. "When he's in trouble, Asteroid Man does this—" The action figure came down right in front of Soldier Mike with a thump that rocked the lap tray and sent coffee sloshing over the side of the cup. "See? He saves him 'cause they're friends."

Carter felt beads of sweat pop out on his forehead as a memory slammed against the barricade he'd built around it. Josh's chatter was muffled by the deafening blast that sucked Carter back in time. He felt the sun-baked ground shudder beneath his feet. Saw a fireball bloom in the distance, reaching so high the flames licked the clouds. By the time he'd reached the scene, two trucks in the convoy had been reduced to smoking metal skeletons.

Along with the buzzing in his ears, Carter had heard shouts and the pop of gunfire from a sniper who'd moved in to finish what the roadside bomb had started.

You'll be nominated for a Silver Star, Wallace.

Carter didn't know why. Sure, he'd saved three men that day. But he'd lost Rob.

His closest friend.

He hadn't reached him in time. And God hadn't bothered to intervene....

Carter was almost relieved when the seat belt sign blinked on a few minutes later and the flight attendant told the passengers the plane would be landing soon. Josh's soldiers retreated to the backpack once again, and he scrambled back to his grandmother's side.

Carter stared out the window as the wheels came down and the plane began its descent. Sheets of gunmetal gray clouds began to unravel, offering a teasing glimpse of the city below. It had been over a year since he'd stepped on Texas soil.

A lifetime ago.

The plane rolled to a stop by the gate, and the child's grandmother smiled at Carter across the aisle. "I can't thank you enough for keeping Josh occupied."

A smile hooked the corner of Carter's lips. "Not a problem, ma'am. Marines are trained to handle all kinds of situations."

"Are you home for good?"

Carter hesitated, not knowing quite how to answer the question. He chose the safest response. "For a little while."

The woman frowned. "But someone will be here to meet you?"

Carter nodded, touched by her concern. "My sister." In her last email, Maddie had promised to pick him up at the Dallas/Fort Worth airport, but that had been several weeks ago and he hadn't been in touch with her since then.

She'd hinted that she had something important to tell him, but insisted the news be shared in person. Carter couldn't imagine what it would be, but there were times he'd been grateful for the distance that separated him from family drama. Besides that, she had Grayson, their older brother, to confide in. The two had always been close, bound together by some invisible thread that Carter had never been able to grab hold of.

There was a flurry of movement around them as the passengers collected their bags. Josh grinned up at him. "Bye."

"Take care, bud," Carter said.

"I will." The boy's thin arms locked around Carter's leg and then he was gone, swallowed up in the line of passengers exiting the plane.

Carter slung the camouflage duffel bag over his shoulder and made his way toward the baggage claim. A businessman glanced up from his laptop and gave him a respectful nod. A woman on the escalator caught his eye and tapped the tiny yellow ribbon pinned to her collar.

Carter had learned that when he wore his uniform, he wasn't just a soldier named Carter Wallace. He was someone's dad. Brother. Son. Across three time zones, people had sought him out. Smiled at him. Thumped him on the back. By touching him, they were touching someone they loved.

It was strange. Humbling.

At the bottom of the escalator, he began to look

for Maddie. She was the kind of woman who stood out in a crowd. Stylish and sophisticated…

"Carter!"

Out of the corner of his eye, a blur of movement began to take shape.

Auburn hair. Big brown eyes…and cowboy boots?

Carter had only a split second to brace himself for impact before Maddie dived into his arms. His throat swelled shut when she clung to him. He couldn't remember his older sister ever being so demonstrative.

"I can't…breathe," he managed.

The choke hold around his neck loosened. A little. "Sorry. It's just—" Were those tears in her eyes? "I'm glad you're here." Sniffling, Maddie stepped back and clasped his shoulders. "Let me look at you."

Carter's lips quirked. "I haven't changed since the last time you saw me."

Not on the outside, anyway.

"You, on the other hand…" His gaze skimmed the Western-style plaid shirt and jeans and paused to linger on her feet. "Nice boots. Are you on some kind of undercover assignment for *Texas Today?*"

"I'll leave the undercover stuff to Gray—and I'm not working at the magazine anymore."

"Not working… I thought you loved your job."

Maddie flashed a wobbly smile. "I told you there have been a lot of changes."

"That's an understatement."

Carter's head whipped around at the sound of a familiar drawl. His brother, Grayson, sauntered up, hand in hand with a beautiful, dark-haired woman and a small boy sporting a cowboy hat and a Dallas Cowboys T-shirt.

Carter had come home on leave several times since he'd enlisted, but he'd never been greeted at the airport by both his siblings before.

"I didn't expect to see you here." He extended his hand but Gray ignored it and hugged him instead, adding a manly thump to his back for good measure.

The lump in Carter's throat doubled in size. Had the plane landed in Fort Worth or *The Twilight Zone?* Because things were getting weirder by the second.

"Carter, I'd like you to meet my fiancée, Elise Lopez, and her son, Cory." Gray smiled down at the woman, an expression on his face that Carter had never seen before. Identical to the one he'd seen on Rob's face whenever he'd talked about Savannah…

He thrust the memory aside.

"Congratulations." Carter glanced at Maddie. "I guess this must be the big news you had to tell me about in person."

A look passed between his siblings.

And that's when Carter felt it. The prickle of unease that skated up his spine and lifted the hairs on the back of his neck. He recognized the signs, similar to the ones he'd experienced trudging through the mountains of Afghanistan.

Suddenly, this no longer felt like a reunion. It felt more like an ambush.

"Let me get this straight. There are *two* of each of you?" Carter leaned forward, staring at his siblings in disbelief.

His *half* siblings, if what Gray had just told him was true.

"We thought it would be better if we waited until you got home to break the news," Maddie said softly.

It would have been better if they hadn't told him at all, Carter thought, still trying to wrap his mind around the fact that his mother, Sharla Wallace, hadn't given birth to Maddie and Gray. They'd spent the past hour explaining that a woman named Belle Colby was their biological mother and both Maddie and Gray had an identical twin.

Which meant their dad had never bothered to mention that he'd been married once before. Brian Wallace might be a distant father—more available to the missionary patients he served than his own family—but he wasn't the kind of man who would keep something like that a secret.

Unless there was a good reason.

Maddie reached for his hand across the kitchen table. At least they'd chosen the privacy of Gray's condo to drop this bomb on him. Gray had left Elise and Cory at Maddie's apartment, where they'd been staying now that his sister was living at the Colby Ranch near a small town named Grasslands.

Carter's older brother was apparently tying up loose ends in Fort Worth before starting his new job at the Grasslands Police Department. Gray and Elise planned on making a permanent move to Grasslands after they were married.

Carter had barely recovered from the news that his brother was engaged when Maddie spilled the rest of the story. Starting with how she'd recently reunited with Violet, her identical twin.

According to Maddie, Violet was the one who'd set things in motion. Her mother, Belle, had been badly injured after falling off a horse last July and she'd set out to find her biological father. A search that had led her to Maddie, instead.

"I know it sounds unbelievable—"

"Unbelievable?" Carter interrupted, shifting just out of Maddie's reach. "How about impossible? You both have an identical twin that you didn't know about. Dad was married before he met Mom.

I think we've gone straight from unbelievable to a guest spot on the Dr. Phil show."

No one smiled. Probably because they knew it was true.

"We've been having a hard time accepting it, too," Gray said carefully. "Unfortunately, Belle can't answer our questions until she comes out of her coma. And...Dad." He stumbled over the word, which suddenly made the story more real than fantasy. Carter wasn't used to seeing his big brother, a tough undercover cop, lose a grip on his emotions. "I'm still trying to track him down."

Carter tried to put himself in Gray's position. While tracing their roots to an old address in Fort Worth, Maddie had met a woman named Patty Earl who'd cast doubts on the fact that Gray and his twin, Jack Colby, were even Brian Wallace's sons. Her late husband, Joe Earl, had claimed that *he'd* fathered the twin boys.

Carter had always felt like the odd man out in his family, but if the woman's claim was true, it meant that he was Brian's only son by blood.

He wanted to talk to his father, demand to know why he'd kept all this a secret. But according to Gray, their dad had disappeared while traveling near the Texas-Mexico border and no one in the family had been able to reach him for several months.

Brian wasn't expected to return until Thanksgiving, but his wallet and cell phone had turned up recently and there was a growing concern that something had happened to him. Another piece of information that Gray and Maddie had waited to tell Carter until he was back in the States.

"I know it's going to take some time to sort all this out," Gray said. "We're still working on it. It's been just as hard on Violet and Jack."

The names meant nothing to Carter. He tried to picture another Maddie. Another Grayson. The "country" equivalents of his big-city sibs. Under different circumstances, the thought would have made him smile.

"I'd like you to meet Ty." Maddie touched the engagement ring on her finger. The last Carter knew, she'd been engaged to Landon Derringer, a Fort Worth CEO who'd been a close friend of the Wallace family for years. Carter was having a hard time keeping up. "And Violet and Jack have invited you to stay at the ranch until we hear from Dad."

"Why?" Frustration sharpened the word but it didn't faze Maddie.

She lifted her chin. "Because family should stick together."

Family? Is that what they were? Because Carter had no idea how to define this tangle of relationships.

"Come on, Carter." Gray met his eyes and Carter

saw a glint of stubbornness there. Or maybe he was seeing his own reflection. "What would it hurt to hang out at the Colby Ranch for a week or two?"

"You'll love it there," Maddie said earnestly. "I promise."

I promise.

Carter's hand closed around the photograph in his pocket.

"Give me a few days."

Maddie's expression clouded. "Carter—"

"There's something I have to do first."

"Did you see the guy who just sat down at table four? Because he sure can't take his eyes off *you*."

"That's your section." Savannah Blackmore brushed aside her coworker's sly comment as she continued to restock the shelves behind the counter.

Libby hadn't been working at the diner very long, so all she knew was that Savannah was single, but not the reason why. Not that it mattered. The "cosmetology student by day—waitress by night" fancied herself a modern-day Emma, matching up people with the hope they would find their own "happily ever after" ending.

Over the past seven months, Savannah had learned there were endings, but they weren't always happy ones.

"He has broad shoulders, too." Libby fanned herself with the order pad.

Some girls noticed a man's smile or the color of his eyes. Libby judged a man by the width of his shoulders. Savannah doubted she could find a pair strong enough to carry her burdens. Guys avoided women with baggage and she had enough to fill up the cargo hold of a Boeing 747. The delicate flutter below her rib cage reminded Savannah there was someone else to consider. Someone *she* needed to be strong for.

That's why she wasn't even tempted to look at the guy at table number four.

"I'll be in the kitchen."

"You can run but you can't hide," her coworker teased.

"Watch me." Savannah made a beeline for the swinging doors that separated the kitchen from the dining area.

Come to think of it, the canned goods in the pantry could use a little organizing, too....

"Order up." Bruce, the diner's owner and self-appointed cook, pointed to a platter piled high with ribs, mashed potatoes drenched in butter and a generous helping of coleslaw.

It was Libby's order, but over the top of the doors, Savannah could see she'd been waylaid by a group of tourists wearing matching T-shirts with the words I Brake For Rodeos emblazoned on the front.

"I'll take it." Savannah grabbed the plate and caught Libby's eye as she rounded the counter. "Where does this one go?"

The impish light that danced in the younger girl's eyes answered Savannah's question even before she could say the words—

"Table four."

With a sigh, Savannah counted the scuffed tiles as she made her way to the back of the diner.

Part of her knew that Libby must have misunderstood the guy's interest. The past few months had taken their toll. She felt—and probably looked—as wrung out as the mop hanging in the utility closet.

Savannah summoned a polite smile as she approached the table.

Okay, so maybe Libby hadn't been exaggerating. The guy's close-cropped hair was the pale gold of winter wheat, a perfect setting for a pair of deep-set, cobalt-blue eyes. A gray T-shirt stretched across the broad shoulders Libby had gone on and on about....

Savannah's gaze locked on the familiar insignia and her mouth went dry.

A soldier.

He rose to his feet as she reached the table. "I'm Sergeant Carter Wallace, ma'am...."

Savannah felt a tingling numbness spread down her arms to her fingertips. The plate wobbled. As a river of barbecue sauce carried the ribs toward the edge, it was gently plucked from her hands and deposited on the table.

The soldier's gaze dropped to the apron tied around her waist, lingering there until Savannah felt the color rise in her cheeks.

What was his problem? Hadn't he seen a pregnant woman before?

"Your waitress will be back in a few minutes to see if you need anything else." Savannah whirled toward the kitchen.

"Savannah? *Wait.*"

How did he know her name?

She slowly turned around, reluctant to face him again.

A muscle worked in the sergeant's jaw. "I know—*knew*—your husband. Rob."

Bitterness and sorrow clashed, splashing over the walls of Savannah's grief. She swallowed hard against the lump that rose in her throat and managed a smile.

"I'm glad one of us did."

Chapter Two

Carter watched Savannah disappear through the swinging doors that separated the kitchen from the dining area.

In his mind, this had played out differently.

Savannah had been happy to see him. Touched by the message that Rob had entrusted him to deliver. Instead, she'd looked at him as if he'd lobbed a grenade in her direction.

Maybe you did.

It occurred to Carter that he shouldn't have chosen a public place to introduce himself, but Rob had never given him their home address, only mentioned the name of the tiny diner in Dallas where Savannah worked.

Carter dropped into the chair again and pressed his fingers against his temples, an attempt to ward off the headache that had sunk its talons behind his eyes. When he'd stepped off the plane, he'd naively assumed that time would slowly begin to sand down the jagged edges of his memories and life would return to normal.

Normal, he remembered his nanny, Rachel, saying with a laugh, *is just a setting on the dryer.*

Carter finally understood what she'd meant. Because so far, nothing had gone the way he'd planned.

He'd spent a sleepless night at Gray's condo, fighting jet lag and the realization that everything he'd believed about his family had been based on a lie.

Breakfast with Maddie and Gray the next morning had been awkward; no one seemed to know how to fill the silence. Carter had politely declined their invitation to church. His brother took off shortly after breakfast to pick up Elise and Cory. After the service, Maddie planned to return to Grasslands so she could check on Belle Colby at the convalescent center.

Carter had welcomed the time alone to regroup. He'd decided to help Gray search for their father, the only person who could tell them the truth about the past. But first, he'd been honor bound to deliver a message.

If the woman the message was intended for decided to cooperate.

"How are those ribs tastin'?" Libby, the waitress

who'd been so attentive when Carter had walked into the diner, bounded up to his table.

"Great." Once Carter tried them, he'd know for sure.

"Okaay." She glanced down at his plate and frowned. "Anything else I can getcha?"

How about an explanation for Savannah's parting words?

I'm glad one of us did.

The statement hadn't made sense. She was Rob's wife. Of course she knew him. Savannah's reaction—and her abrupt departure—didn't quite match up with the woman Rob had described. A woman with a sweet smile, a sense of humor and a strong faith.

Carter understood how grief could do a number on someone, but wouldn't she want to talk to someone who'd spent time with Rob?

Been with him at the end?

His gaze shifted to the kitchen, where Savannah was hiding out. If he could outlast a sniper for ten hours, he could certainly wait out a pretty green-eyed waitress.

"I'll take a piece of pie and a cup of coffee."

Libby followed the direction of his eyes and grinned. "Coming right up."

A half hour ticked by and the dining room emptied as the lunch crowd dwindled. Carter finished off the pie and started on his third cup of coffee but there was still no sign of Savannah.

"Excuse me?" He motioned to Libby as she emerged from the kitchen, armed with two coffee pots. She changed direction, navigating through the maze of tables until she reached his side.

"Do you need a warm up on that coffee?"

He needed to talk to Savannah. "No, thanks. Just the bill." Carter reached for his wallet. "Is Savannah busy?" he tossed out casually.

"No." The smile dimmed. "She left a little while ago."

"Left?"

"She said she wasn't feeling well."

Savannah had slipped past him. Admiration and frustration battled for dominance. Frustration won.

Carter released a slow breath. "Will she be back tomorrow?"

"She's not scheduled to work again until Tuesday."

Great. Before she'd left, Maddie made him promise he would drive to Grasslands to meet the rest of the "family" as soon as possible.

"Would you mind giving me her home address?"

Libby looked uneasy with the request. "I don't know—"

"Her husband and I served together in Afghanistan. He introduced us." It was the truth. Sort of. He and Savannah might not have met until today, but Carter felt as if he knew her. He knew that she hummed when she was nervous and that her favorite color was blue. She liked yellow roses and coffee-flavored ice cream and black-and-white movies.

And she was more beautiful in person than she was in the photograph Rob had given him.

Carter set that thought firmly to the side.

"I didn't know Savannah was married to a soldier," Libby breathed. "She never talks about him."

"He talked about her." Twenty-four seven. "And he asked me to deliver a message."

"That's *so* romantic."

Only in the movies, Carter wanted to say. The reality hadn't been quite so warm and fuzzy.

He and Rob had been shoulder to shoulder in a shallow ditch, caught in the middle of a firefight. Under attack from both the ground and the air.

If anything happens to me, promise that you'll find Savannah and make sure she's okay. Tell her that I loved her.

But Rob hadn't told him that Savannah might not *want* to be found.

Or that she was pregnant.

"Going somewhere?"

Savannah whirled around at the sound of a deep male voice.

It was him. Carter Wallace. The soldier who'd shown up at the diner that morning. He filled the doorway, arms folded across his chest in a casually deceptive stance. The set of his jaw warned Savannah that she wouldn't evade him as easily this time.

She didn't bother to ask how he'd found out where she lived. He must have sweet-talked Libby after she'd left the diner.

"Your landlady let me in." Those intense blue eyes scanned the living room and narrowed on the hedge of cardboard boxes that separated them.

"Look, Sergeant Wallace." Savannah heard a catch in her voice. "I don't know what you want—"

"That's because you didn't wait around long enough to find out." The corners of his lips kicked up in a rueful smile. "I'm sorry if I upset you when I showed up at the diner today. Rob told me where you worked but not your address."

Rob told him.

Savannah's throat tightened. She couldn't deal with this right now. Not when she'd spent the past few hours packing up her things, each box she taped shut one more reminder that she was closing the door on the past with no idea what the future would bring.

"Do you mind if I come in?"

Yes, she did.

"I'm really busy." To prove it, Savannah bent down and snatched up one of the boxes. A muscle in her lower back protested the suddenness of the movement and she winced in pain.

"Hey—take it easy." Carter Wallace was at her side in an instant and he plucked the box from her hands. "Should you be lifting stuff?"

Color flooded Savannah's cheeks when she saw his gaze drop to her rounded stomach, something that even a loose-fitting sweatshirt couldn't hide.

"I'm not an invalid." She was just…tired. And not prepared for unexpected company. Especially a handsome, blue-eyed soldier who'd claimed to be friends with her late husband.

"Where do you want this?" Carter stared her down.

Good job, Savannah. Instead of convincing him to leave, she'd unwittingly given him a reason to stay.

"Really, you don't have to—" She saw his eyebrows dip together and realized there was no point in arguing. "By the door."

Without a word, Carter strode across the room and deposited it near the entryway. And then proceeded to do the same with the rest of the boxes.

As he set the last one down, Savannah didn't miss his swift but thorough assessment of the cramped upstairs apartment she'd briefly shared with Rob after their wedding.

"Thank you." Savannah glanced at her watch, hoping Carter would take the hint.

He did.

"I'll only take up a few minutes of your time," he said quietly. "It's important."

Savannah sighed. Maybe the best thing was to get this over with as quickly as possible and send Sergeant Wallace on his way.

"All right." She motioned toward a chair and sent up a swift, silent prayer for strength as Carter sat down. The flimsy wood creaked under the weight of his solid frame, the floral slipcover an almost comical backdrop for a guy who looked as if he could bench press the sofa.

It didn't matter that Carter Wallace wasn't in full uniform. His faded, loose-fitting jeans and a gray T-shirt with the marine insignia that stretched across his muscular chest proved to be just as intimidating. He looked as if he were born to be a soldier.

Savannah perched on the edge of the sofa and waited. But now that he had her attention, Carter didn't seem to know what to say.

"You mentioned that you knew Rob—" Savannah's voice cracked as grief sliced at the threads of her composure. She'd barely begun to accept the fact that her husband had walked out on their marriage when a military chaplain had knocked at the door and informed her that Rob had been killed in a roadside bombing.

Carter nodded. "He was assigned to my unit. We worked together. He talked about you."

Savannah's fingers knotted together in her lap. "He did?"

Carter looked surprised by the question. "All the time." He paused. "That's why I'm here. A few days before Rob… He asked me to give you a message."

Savannah heard a rushing sound in her ears. Spots began to dance in front of her eyes. "A message?"

This wasn't what she'd expected. She'd assumed that Carter had sought her out because Rob had owed him money. After the funeral, she'd received calls from some of his former buddies, asking if she would "make good" on the loans they'd given him.

Each one a reminder of how gullible she'd been.

"He was a good man. A good friend." Carter leaned forward. "And he…he loved you."

Savannah felt the color drain from her face. "You don't know what you're talking about."

Carter frowned. "That's the message that Rob asked me to deliver. He wanted me to tell you that he loved you."

Savannah's breath collected in her lungs, making it difficult to breathe.

"Sergeant Wallace, Rob *left* me."

Carter stared at Savannah, more shaken by the words than he let on. Rob hadn't mentioned that Savannah didn't support his decision to become a soldier.

"To serve his country, yes," he said carefully. "Rob thought he was doing the right thing, but he couldn't wait to finish his tour and come home to you. It was all he talked about."

Savannah vaulted from the chair and then swayed on her feet. For a split second, Carter was afraid she was going to pass out. Instinctively, he reached out to steady her but she spun away from him, one hand pressed protectively against her belly, the other one palm up, as if trying to keep him at a distance.

"Please. Just go."

Carter sucked in a breath, the flash of pain in those green eyes landing with the force of a physical blow. It was obvious that Savannah was still grieving. He fumbled for the right words, something that had never come easily. Unlike Rob, who'd entertained everyone on base with his anecdotes.

"Savannah, I know this must be difficult. Have you talked to someone—"

"I didn't mean that Rob left when he enlisted. I meant that he left *me.* A week after we were married," she choked out. "He sent one letter when he finished basic training saying that he'd made a… mistake. After that, I never heard from him again."

The words hit Carter broadside. "I don't understand."

"I think you do." Savannah's gaze didn't waver. "You just don't believe me."

Carter opened his mouth, ready to argue, and then realized she was right. What Savannah had just told him clashed with the man that Carter knew. The one who'd been devoted to his wife.

Rob had bragged about their plans for the future. Buying a piece of land. Building a home. Raising a family.

Why would—

Carter's heart plummeted to the soles of his boots, weighted down by a sudden, unwelcome suspicion. "The baby—"

Emerald sparks flashed in Savannah's eyes. "Is Rob's. But he…he never knew."

"You didn't tell him?" Carter regretted the question the moment Savannah started toward the door.

To see him out.

But Carter didn't move. Wasn't going to move until he got some answers. "Rob never mentioned that you were separated. In fact, all he talked about were the things the two of you were going to do when his tour ended."

"Then he lied to you, too."

Too?

The band around Carter's forehead tightened. "Rob and I were friends. Why would he do that?"

He had looked up to Rob. Admired him.

Envied him.

Carter had dodged serious relationships for years, never going out with the same woman more than once or twice. Knowing how hard it had been on him and his siblings every time their father left on a mission trip, he was determined not to subject someone he cared about to a relationship marked by uncertainty and goodbyes. Something the wife of a soldier had to accept. But listening to Rob talk about Savannah had made him question his decision to remain single. Made him wonder what it would be like to have a woman like her in his life.

Now she was trying to convince him that it had all been a lie?

Savannah opened the door, which didn't answer his question but guaranteed there wouldn't be an opportunity to ask any more.

Carter didn't know what—or who—to believe. Savannah? A woman he'd just met. Or Rob, the guy who'd laughed with him? Encouraged him to pray, even though every mile Carter had hiked through the rugged hills of Afghanistan had taken him that much farther from the faith he'd professed as a child?

The guy that Savannah claimed had abandoned her.

What he *did* know was that she wanted him to leave.

"I'm sorry," Carter muttered, although he wasn't quite sure why he was apologizing. Or even who he was apologizing *to*. "I won't take up any more of your time."

As he started to move past her, she touched his arm. A gesture that stopped Carter in his tracks.

"Sergeant Wallace? Thank you for keeping your promise," she whispered. "I am… I'm glad that Rob had a friend over there."

The words brought Carter up short. He had kept his promise—but not all of it.

Find Savannah and make sure she's okay.

For the first time, he noticed the lavender shadows below her eyes. Being the youngest in the family, Carter didn't have a lot of experience with kids, but he figured that working at a diner wouldn't be easy on a pregnant woman.

Savannah's grief might be coloring her perspective about Rob's feelings for her—maybe she'd somehow misinterpreted the reason he'd left—but Carter couldn't simply walk out the door until he knew that she wasn't alone.

"Are you moving back home?" he asked abruptly.

"Home?"

"Back to your family."

"I'm staying in Dallas." An emotion Carter couldn't identify flickered in Savannah's eyes. "But my landlady's nephew needed a place to stay so she asked me to find something else."

She was being *evicted?*

"Don't you have a lease?"

"Mrs. Cabera only agreed to let me stay here because Rob and her son had gone to high school together. It was a verbal agreement."

Carter didn't like the sound of that. "But you have somewhere to go, right?"

Savannah hesitated just long enough to make him suspicious. "Of course."

"Where?"

Her pink lips compressed. "This isn't your problem."

In a roundabout way, that answered his question.

"What are your plans?"

Savannah was silent for so long that Carter didn't think she was going to answer the question.

"I'll check into a hotel for a few days. Until I find something else," she finally said.

"Isn't there a family member who can put you up for a while?"

"No."

Funny how one simple word could complicate a situation, Carter thought.

"Well, I happen to have picked up a few extras recently," he said lightly. "And one of them owns a ranch near Grasslands. My sister, Maddie, offered me one of the empty cottages on the property, but you can stay there—"

Savannah's eyes widened and Carter felt a slow burn crawl up his neck when he realized how that sounded. "—and I can bunk in the main house," he added quickly. "You'd have a place to rest up. Until you find something else."

Color swept into Savannah's cheeks, filling the faint hollows beneath her cheekbones.

"That's very nice of you." She regarded him warily, as if she wasn't sure it was nice of him at all. "But I can't just quit my job at the diner. And I'm sure that when your sister offered you a place to stay, she wasn't expecting you to pass it on to a random stranger."

Carter could have argued the point. Savannah wasn't a stranger. He'd carried her photograph around in his pocket for the past two months. Memorized the heart-shaped face and delicate features.

But how could he tell her that without coming across as some kind of stalker?

"I heard someone say that sometimes, a change of scenery can change your perspective."

Carter decided not to mention Rob was the one who'd told him that.

For a moment it looked as if Savannah was wavering. But then her chin came up and Carter saw the answer in her eyes.

"You don't have to worry about me. I know you were Rob's friend, but I'm not your responsibility."

Find Savannah and make sure she's okay.

Whether Carter wanted it to or not, that *made* her his responsibility.

"But it's not just you anymore, is it?" he reminded her. "You have your baby to think of, too."

Savannah flinched. "Goodbye, Sergeant Wallace."

Carter battled his rising frustration, not sure how to get through to her. "When I make a promise, I keep it."

"And you did. You delivered Rob's message—"

"Not that promise." Carter interrupted. "I'm a marine, ma'am. And we never leave a man—or a woman—behind."

Even though he was serious, Carter flashed a smile, letting her know that she could trust him.

A smile Savannah didn't return.

"You aren't leaving me behind, sergeant." The door began to close. "I'm *asking* you to go."

Chapter Three

"So, when will you be here?"

Carter sighed into the phone as he entered the post office. "Soon."

"How soon?" Maddie wanted to know.

"A few more days." Long enough to give Savannah time to change her mind.

Carter had jotted his cell phone number and the Colby Ranch's address on a piece of paper and tucked it under the windshield wiper of her car after she'd shut the door in his face the day before.

He hadn't been able to stop thinking about her. Wondering what had happened between her and Rob. None of the things Savannah had told him lined up with the claims his friend had made, but Carter couldn't shake the feeling that *she* was the one who'd been telling the truth. Unsettling, given the fact he'd trusted Rob with his life.

"Jack said he might be able to find some work

for you around the ranch now that you're out of the service," Maddie continued. "You love being outdoors. You helped Dad build that playhouse in the backyard when we lived in Appleton, remember? Once it was finished, you told everyone that you wanted to live there. I had to lure you into the house with chocolate chip cookies when it was bedtime."

Maddie's low laugh flowed over him, stirring up memories from the past.

Carter remembered handing his dad the nails, one by one. It was one of the few times they'd actually worked on a project together. Once his dad had started medical school, he'd left Rachel, the full-time nanny he'd hired, in charge of the family. Carter had heard the words "don't bother your father" so often over the next few years, he'd eventually taken them to heart.

"I'll come to Grasslands and meet Violet and Jack—" Carter still couldn't think of them as family. "But I can't promise any more than that right now."

"I just want us to be together," Maddie whispered. "With Dad gone..."

Dad is always gone, Carter was tempted to say. He knew that Gray and Maddie were concerned that something bad might have happened to their father, but knowing Brian, he'd probably just got caught up in his work and assumed everything back home was fine. Thanksgiving, the day he'd promised he would be home, was still three weeks away.

Gray had explained they couldn't file a missing person's report because technically, Brian Wallace wasn't considered missing.

"I'll be there." Carter inserted the key into the post office box he'd kept in the city. "By the weekend—" A package tumbled out with an avalanche of junk mail. He winced as it hit the tiled floor. "I hope that wasn't something breakable," he muttered.

Maddie heard him. "Breakable? Where are you?"

"I'm at the post office and there's a package in here that didn't get forwarded for some reason."

"A package," Maddie repeated. "What does it look like?"

"Um…like a package?"

"Well, open it!"

Carter rolled his eyes. Bossy older sisters. But there was a tension in Maddie's voice that hadn't been there before. Not even when she'd been pestering him about coming to Grasslands. He dumped the letters onto a nearby counter and cut through the tape on the package with his pocketknife.

"Did you send this?" Carter stared at the small,

leather-bound book swaddled in tissue paper. "Because I already have one."

Not that he'd cracked it open for a few years.

"What is it?" Maddie whispered.

"A Bible."

"Is there a note inside?"

Carter thumbed through the delicate, gold-tipped pages and found a piece of paper. "How did you know?"

"Because someone sent a Bible to me and Gray. And to Violet and Jack."

Carter quickly skimmed the contents of the letter and then read it out loud.

"'I'm sorry for what I did to you and your family. I hope you and your siblings can find it in your hearts to forgive me.'"

It wasn't signed.

"What is this about? Who sent it?"

"We don't know," Maddie admitted. "At first we assumed it was a mistake because whoever wrote the other letters specifically mentioned a twin. But Gray thinks it might have something to do with the reason we were separated."

"Maybe it has something to do with Dad's disappearance." Carter read through the words a second time, trying to make sense of the cryptic message. "Why didn't you mention this before?"

"We didn't think you'd—" Maddie stopped.

"Get one." Carter filled in the blanks.

Because at the moment, he was the only one in the Wallace-Colby puzzle who actually knew where he fit. Which, the irony wasn't lost on Carter, made him the odd man out. Again.

"I'm sorry, Carter." Maddie sounded on the verge of tears now. "Gray will want to see the letter and compare the handwriting, but it has to be from the same person. Maybe if we put all of them together, we'll find something that we missed."

Carter held back a sigh.

"I'm on my way."

"I have to admit I'm not happy with the numbers I'm seeing this morning."

Savannah felt a stab of fear as Dr. Yardley set the paperwork down on the desk and took a seat across from her in the examining room.

"Is there something wrong with the baby?"

"The baby seems to be fine. It's *you* I'm worried about," the doctor said bluntly. "Your blood pressure is elevated, and you've actually lost weight since your last appointment."

"I'm feeling fine," Savannah protested. "A little tired, that's all."

"Mmm." Dr. Yardley looked skeptical. "How many hours did you work at the diner last week?"

Savannah silently tallied them up. "Between twenty-five and thirty." Give or take a few. She'd volunteered to cover for one of the waitresses who was standing up in a friend's wedding so she would have money to cover the security deposit on a new apartment.

The apartment she still hadn't found.

After being on her feet all day, she just couldn't seem to summon the energy to search for a new place to live. Savannah assumed it was normal to feel this way but the concern in the doctor's eyes told her otherwise.

"That's what I thought." Dr. Yardley shook her head. "I want you to cut back to half that amount. Effective when you walk out of this office today."

"But I promised my boss that I could fill in on weekends and evenings when I wasn't working my regular shift." Savannah stared at her obstetrician in dismay. "It was the only reason he hired me."

"You've been under a tremendous amount of stress throughout this pregnancy, Savannah, and you still have three months to go. If you end up on complete bed rest, you won't be able to work at all." The doctor's stern words were tempered with a smile. "You need more rest and a little TLC. Two things that I'm afraid modern medicine hasn't figured out how to put in a pill yet."

Savannah laced her fingers together in her lap to stop them from shaking. "I'll talk to him." Although Bruce didn't exactly have a reputation for his easygoing disposition.

The doctor gave her a shrewd look. "Is there anything else going on that I should know about?"

"I've been looking for a new apartment," Savannah admitted. "But I'm sure that I'll find something in the next few days."

Dr. Yardley's pen tapped the clipboard. "Isn't there a family member you can stay with until the baby is born?"

"I don't have any family." One of the reasons she'd been so quick to fall for Rob's charm.

"All right, then. How about a friend?" the physician persisted.

Even as Savannah was shaking her head, an image of Carter Wallace's face flashed through her mind.

No. Way.

She didn't want to accept his help. Carter had been stunned when she'd told him that Rob had left her. Savannah hadn't really expected him to believe her word over Rob's—but still, it had hurt. Why, she wasn't sure.

She wasn't sure why Carter had offered her a place to stay on his sister's ranch near Grasslands, either. The sergeant had been Rob's friend. She, on the other hand, was simply an obligation. One he had probably been relieved to cross off his list. There was no way she was going to show up on his doorstep like an orphan puppy in search of a home.

She'd viewed Rob as a knight in shining armor,

swooping in to rescue her, and look where she was now. A single mother on the verge of being homeless.

God, I know that I'm not alone. I know that You're with me. Show me what I'm supposed to do.

"I know things are difficult right now, but you have to do what's best for you and the baby," Dr. Yardley was saying. "If I could, I'd write you a prescription for a change of scenery. I think that's what you need more than anything right now."

A change of scenery can give you a change in perspective.

The words chased through her mind, stirring the memory of someone else who had said the same thing.

Savannah didn't know whether to laugh or cry. Because even though she'd just asked God to show her what to do, she wasn't ready to acknowledge that Carter Wallace just might be the answer to her prayer.

"Earth to Carter. Come in, Carter."

Maddie's teasing voice yanked Carter back to the present.

"Sorry." He cocked his head to one side. "Reception is still a little fuzzy between earth and *The Twilight Zone*."

Laughter rippled through the dining room and once again, Carter had to adjust to the sound. To the faces of the people gathered around the long plank table. Gray and Jack. Violet and Maddie. Identical but…not.

"What's *The Twilight Zone?*" Eight-year-old Darcy Garland's lively, brown-eyed gaze bounced back and forth between the adults.

"It's not real," Ty Garland, the little girl's father, explained. Carter saw him wink at Maddie across the table.

Yeah. That was another thing. His siblings hadn't only found each other, they'd found, in Maddie's words, "their soul mates." Carter was still trying to wrap his brain around that, too.

"That's what you think," Jack Colby muttered. "You don't have to get used to a guy walking around with *your* face."

"Wearing a shirt and tie," Violet added, her eyes dancing with mischief.

"She's right." Jack flashed a wicked grin in Gray's direction. "When you start working for the Grasslands Police department in January, Sheriff Cole will have you trading in those fancy city duds for a pair of Levis and Tony Lamas in no time."

Their easy banter ricocheted around the table and Carter felt a stab of envy. Violet and Jack Colby had gone out of their way to make him feel welcome since his arrival, but Carter still felt as if his life had become a jigsaw puzzle in which the pieces no longer fit together.

But at least he *had* family. More than he was comfortable with, at the moment.

Carter's gaze drifted to the window. Again.

Almost a week had gone by since he'd left the city and he still couldn't stop thinking about Savannah.

He lay awake at night, scrolling through past conversations with his friend. Searching for scraps of information that verified what Savannah had told him. Rob had talked about her constantly… but had he ever talked *to* her? Sent an email or letter? Received one?

That's what Carter couldn't remember.

Lupita Ramirez, the ranch cook and housekeeper, bustled into the dining room. She rapped a wooden spoon against the palm of her hand to get everyone's attention.

"Who has room for chocolate cake?"

A collective groan followed the question.

"No one—" Jack started to say.

"But we'll take some anyway," Maddie and Violet sang out. At the same time. And then they laughed. In unison.

"Weird," Ty Garland muttered.

Carter had to agree.

"I'm going to have to start working out more." Gray sighed when the housekeeper left the dining room. "Lupita makes enough food to feed the entire county."

"That reminds me, Pastor Jeb wants the church to host a special harvest dinner the weekend before Thanksgiving," Violet said. "He's been calling around, asking members of the congregation to volunteer to help, but he wants to invite the whole community."

Unbidden, an image of Savannah's face swept into Carter's mind. Again. The flash of anger in those expressive green eyes when he'd asked about the baby. The vulnerable curve of her lower lip.

Did she have plans for Thanksgiving? Or would she be alone?

Carter shifted in the chair. In his mind's eye, he could see her standing by the door, arms wrapped protectively around her middle. Proud. *Scared.*

She made it pretty clear that she isn't your concern, he reminded himself.

But that didn't stop him from wondering how she was doing. Had she found an apartment yet? He hated to think of her staying in a hotel with a baby on the way, even for a few days.

Carter had made Rob two promises before his friend had died. He'd promised that he would always have Rob's back and he'd promised that he would make sure Savannah was okay. So far, he hadn't kept either one of them.

"I'll see if I can't round up a few of the boys from the teen center to help with setup or something," Landon Derringer was saying. "They're always complaining they don't have anything to do."

"Round up?" Violet grinned at her fiancé's choice of words. "You're starting to think like a cowboy already, sweetheart."

Gray shook his head in mock sorrow. "Another victim."

Across the table, Derringer smiled at Violet, confirmation that he'd been a willing one.

Carter had been stunned to find Landon, Maddie's former fiancé, at the ranch when he'd arrived. The guy had followed his sister to Grasslands and fallen in love with...Violet. And apparently no one but Carter thought that was strange. But in light of the other things the family had experienced lately, maybe it hadn't even made the list.

"I think a harvest dinner is a great idea." Violet handed a pitcher of cream to Maddie a second before she reached for it. "We have a lot to be thankful for."

Carter couldn't believe a murmur of agreement followed the statement. Maybe if they'd witnessed some of the things that he had over the past five years, they would have a different perspective. And given what they'd been through lately with Belle's accident and Brian's disappearance, Carter didn't think there was a whole lot to be thankful for, either.

Maddie's expression turned pensive but she

smiled at Violet. "This is the first Thanksgiving we'll all be together."

"Mom loves holidays," Violet said wistfully. "She pulls out all the stops.... I know she'll be home by then. She *has* to be."

"There are a lot of people praying for her," Maddie whispered.

But Carter noticed that everyone sidestepped the real question. Whether his father would be in attendance. Carter had managed to corner Gray for a few minutes and his brother had finally admitted how worried he was that something had happened to Brian. Their dad ministered to transient people in remote areas along the border, and the last person Gray had been in contact with had noticed that he seemed ill. Carter tried to convince himself that a physician would certainly know what to do—where to go—if he came down with something.

Unless he was alone and didn't have access to the medicine he needed to fight the illness. His dad's cell phone had been recovered a few weeks ago, but there were other ways he could have maintained contact with the rest of the family. Why hadn't he used them?

Carter felt the walls begin to close in and suddenly felt the need for some fresh air.

"No dessert for me." His chair scraped the floor as he rose to his feet. "I think I'll take a walk."

"Sure." Maddie frowned.

So did Violet.

Carter blinked but there were still two of them. Oh, yeah. He definitely needed some fresh air.

He could feel everyone watching as he walked out of the dining room. The second the door closed, he would be the next topic of conversation around the dinner table.

Carter wasn't used to that, either. His older siblings valued and encouraged independence. Other than exchanging brief updates now and then, Maddie and Gray had pursued their own interests and left him alone. Carter wasn't quite sure what to do with the sudden interest they were showing now. Add Jack and Violet into the mix, and Carter was beginning to feel like it was four against one. Odds he didn't care for.

He stepped outside, back against the door as he made a swift but thorough sweep of the property. Searching for possible threats.

You're in Texas, remember?

It took a moment to let his soul adjust to the newness of his surroundings. The rustle of the wind through the pecan grove. The scent of the mesquite trees. Miles of blue sky. A place that Maddie and Gray were both ready to call home.

And yet Carter was tempted to reenlist after they located his dad. In the military, he knew exactly who he was. What he was supposed to do. Now, it felt as if he'd stripped of his identity along with his uniform.

Nipper, Jack's Australian shepherd, bounded up to him, and Carter reached down to scratch the dog's velvety ears.

"I suppose you want to go for a walk?" Roaming the property together had become a nightly ritual when Carter couldn't sleep.

The dog's tail slashed the air and he barked. Carter took that as a yes.

Restlessness drove him toward the creek where the cottages were located. In spite of Violet's generous offer, Carter had decided to stay in the main house and bunk in the guest room that Gray occupied when he visited the ranch, leaving one of the cottages empty in case Savannah changed her mind. A possibility that had begun to shrink over the past few days.

Savannah hadn't exactly welcomed him with open arms. What made him think she would accept his help?

Just as Carter reached the creek bank, his cell phone rang.

An unfamiliar number appeared on the screen and Carter's heart slammed against his rib cage. Had his father finally discovered they'd been trying to contact him?

"Hello?"

He heard a crackling sound. And then a tentative but familiar voice. "Hi."

"Savannah?"

"Yes." A long pause followed. "I hope I'm not interrupting anything."

"Not at all." Carter's hand tightened around the phone. "Is everything all right?"

"I'm sorry I didn't—" The line crackled, distorting her words. If they lost the connection, Carter was afraid she wouldn't call back.

"Savannah? You're breaking up. Where are you?"

"I'm…here."

"Here?" Carter repeated.

"At the gate."

Chapter Four

Savannah's heart performed a little Texas two-step as Carter Wallace approached.

In faded jeans and a long-sleeved black T-shirt that accentuated his athletic build, Carter was even more attractive than she remembered. His loose-limbed stride and the set of his broad shoulders conveyed the fierce confidence of a man who faced life head-on. A confidence Savannah couldn't help but envy.

Once again, she contemplated turning the car around. Something that had crossed her mind at least half a dozen times since she'd left Dallas.

Her boss hadn't exactly been thrilled when she'd stopped by the diner after her appointment with Dr. Yardley and told him that she had to reduce her hours. The next day, when Savannah checked the schedule, she saw that not only had Bruce honored her request, he'd given *all* her shifts to a new waitress he'd hired over the weekend.

Leaving her with no choice but to accept Carter's offer to stay at his sister's ranch for the time being.

But doubts began to creep in as Savannah parked between the massive stone columns that stood like sentinels on either side of the driveway, guarding the property from outsiders. Like her. She wasn't sure what she'd expected, but the Colby Ranch was obviously a large, prosperous operation.

It only reminded Savannah how little she knew about Carter Wallace. Was she really welcome here? Maybe he was already regretting his impulsive invitation.

Rob had made a lot of promises, too, and he'd only kept one of them.

I'm leaving, Savannah.

Savannah's fingers closed around the shift stick but the passenger-side door opened before she could put the car in reverse. Carter hopped in beside her, his large frame folding almost in half to accommodate the passenger seat of her compact car.

Savannah took a deep breath. If he looked at her with pity, she'd turn the car around and head straight back to Dallas....

"It's about time." The crooked smile that Carter

flashed in her direction coaxed a dimple out of hiding, an unexpected but charming contrast to the man's ruggedly handsome features. "If you didn't show up within the next twenty-four hours, I'd decided to round up a posse and find you."

He'd planned to return to Dallas? For her?

No, not for you. For Rob, she reminded herself sternly. An internal dash of cold water on the warmth his words stirred in her heart.

It would be a mistake to forget the reason she was here. To Carter, delivering Rob's message had been a duty. An obligation. But Savannah had an obligation, too. To do everything she could to protect the health of her unborn child. Even if it meant swallowing her pride and accepting help from a stranger.

"I hope this isn't a bad time," she stammered. "I probably should have called first."

Except that if she'd dialed Carter's number any earlier, Savannah knew she would have lost not only her voice, but her nerve. She'd packed her suitcase that morning and stowed it in the trunk of the car, giving God what she hoped was ample opportunity to send some kind of sign that He had another plan. One that *didn't* include Carter Wallace.

Yet here she was.

"I didn't call before I showed up at your door

that day, either," Carter said easily. "So I guess that makes us even."

No, they weren't. Not until he understood that she didn't intend to be a charity case or outstay her welcome here. She'd scheduled another appointment with Dr. Yardley in two weeks. If the test results proved that she was obeying orders, Savannah planned to ask for an increase in her hours at the diner again and continue her search for another apartment.

"I can pay rent." Savannah didn't look at Carter as she put the car into gear and continued down the long gravel driveway. "I don't expect to live in the cottage for free. Or I can help out around the house or in the kitchen. I'm a pretty decent cook."

At one time, she'd dreamed of attending culinary school. Before she'd met Rob.

"Chicken and dumplings are your specialty, right?"

"How did you know..." Savannah's voice trailed off, leaving an awkward silence in its wake.

Rob must have told him.

The day they'd met, Carter had claimed that Rob talked about her all the time when they'd served together in Afghanistan. Savannah hadn't believed him—until now. The thought that Rob's friend knew more about her than she knew about him was a little unsettling.

And what else had Rob told him? The truth—or

more lies? Less than twenty-four hours after they were married, Savannah had discovered that her new husband didn't seem to know the difference. She'd been so tired of being alone that she'd let Rob sweep her off her feet.

Believed everything he'd said…

"Don't worry about things like paying rent or washing dishes right now." Savannah could feel the weight of Carter's gaze, studying her profile. "How about I show you where you'll be staying first? You can unpack your things. Settle in and get a good night's sleep."

Which could only be, Savannah thought ruefully, a tactful way of saying that she must look as exhausted as she felt.

"All right." Self-consciously, she looped a wayward strand of hair behind her ear. She knew the past few days had taken a toll on both her health and her emotions. The stress of apartment hunting during the day. Wrestling with her fears at night. Savannah had been reading through the New Testament every morning, taking comfort in the fact that other believers had faced difficult situations, too, and God hadn't abandoned them.

She trusted Him. Men, not so much anymore.

"Keep going past the main house," Carter instructed.

The simple description didn't do the place justice.

Savannah tried not to gawk as they passed a magnificent two-story home fashioned from native stone and brick. The setting sun winked off the mullioned windows and painted the glass with a rosy, welcoming glow. Trumpet vine wove through the spindles of the wrought-iron fence that separated the landscaped lawn from the rest of the property.

Everything was neat and well cared for. The Colby Ranch could have easily been featured on the cover of *Texas Today* magazine.

"It's beautiful," Savannah murmured. "Did you grow up here?"

"No."

Savannah tried not to flinch at the sting of Carter's curt response. Although he seemed to know a lot about her, it was becoming clear that Carter wasn't going to be very forthcoming about his own life.

Carter saw Savannah's hands tighten around the steering wheel and realized the word had come out a little sharper than he'd intended. He tried again.

"No," he said more softly.

One-syllable words were okay on a military base, but if he wanted Savannah to stay at the ranch, it was clear to Carter that he would have to brush up on his people skills. He could coax a disabled vehicle back to life and make an engine purr like a kitten, but he'd never been much for small talk.

Especially when the woman sitting next to him took his breath away.

The photograph hadn't done her justice. Savannah's honey-brown hair fell loose around her shoulders, a perfect frame for her delicate features and wide green eyes.

The only thing missing was the smile.

Carter still hadn't seen one of those.

When he'd heard her voice on the phone, he couldn't believe that Savannah had actually accepted his invitation. Not until he'd spotted her car parked at the gate. Both hands gripping the steering wheel, ready to turn around and exit his life as quickly as she'd entered it.

He wasn't sure why Savannah had changed her mind, but now that she was here at the Colby Ranch, Carter was going to make sure she stuck around for a while.

It's what Rob would have wanted.

Carter was certain about that, no matter what Savannah had said about their marriage. Why would Rob fake devotion to a wife that he'd abandoned? What would he have to gain?

Savannah might need a place to stay, but Carter

needed some answers. And the woman sitting next to him was the only one who could provide them.

Another light winked on in the house. Carter hoped no one would glance out the window and see an unfamiliar vehicle nudging its way up the drive. Typically after Lupita served dessert, everyone pitched in and cleaned up from dinner and then gathered in the family room to watch a movie or play a game. Ty and Maddie would help Darcy with her homework. Jack and Gray would take part in what had become their favorite pastime—giving each other a hard time—while the women planned their upcoming nuptials with all the intensity of a military strategist.

And they insisted he join them.

Bonding, Maddie called it. Carter figured it was easier to bond with people who shared your DNA. He'd never had much in common with his siblings before, and now he was no longer sure he and Gray had *that* in common.

Carter would count the seconds until he could come up with a reasonable excuse to slip away. But now, for the first time, he hoped they followed standard protocol again and did not show up at the cottage to meet the newest visitor. It might overwhelm Savannah and give her a reason to bolt.

She didn't trust him, that much was clear.

But Rob had. Which meant that Carter was

honor bound to shield her from potentially stressful situations.

Meeting his family definitely qualified.

Savannah fixed her eyes on the driveway.

The sudden drop in temperature inside the car made her wonder if there was some family dynamic going on between Carter and his sister that she should know about. The last thing she wanted was for her presence to add tension to an already strained relationship.

"You can take the first right behind the barn." Carter pointed to an enormous metal building with a green roof. Two chestnut horses stood shoulder to shoulder in a corner of the paddock, dozing under the branches of a cottonwood tree.

Savannah followed his instructions and saw a row of adorable little cottages scattered along a creek bed.

"I've been staying in the main house but the cottage on the end is empty. My sister had it all made up for me, but I never moved in. That means it's all yours," Carter said.

Yours.

In spite of her misgivings, the word flowed through Savannah, as sweet as a glass of tea on a hot summer day. Even knowing this was a temporary arrangement couldn't prevent the sense of wonder that swept over her.

The branches of two mature pecan trees formed a canopy over a cottage as whimsical as an illustration in a child's storybook. A sloping roof with patchwork shingles shaded an enclosed porch like the brim of a hat. Narrow wooden shutters trimmed the windows. Blue. Her favorite color. A hand-woven basket, overflowing with gourds and miniature pumpkins, sat on the top step like a welcome gift.

An Australian shepherd emerged from one of the outbuildings and ambled toward the car as Savannah pulled up in front of the cottage.

"That's Nipper. Jack Colby's dog." Carter shook his head. "Don't let the name fool you, though. The only thing that mutt might do is lick you to death."

"Is Jack part of your family?"

"That's the question of the day," he muttered.

Savannah frowned. "I don't understand."

But Carter didn't bother to enlighten her. Instead, he hopped out and jogged around the front of the car to open her door. His large hand gently cupped her elbow as he helped her out of the vehicle.

The warmth of his touch sparked something that sent Savannah's blood racing through her veins like a prairie fire.

She sucked in a breath, yanked her heart back in line.

It wasn't as if she were...*attracted*...to Carter Wallace. More than likely sleepless nights and low blood sugar had tipped her off balance.

Guard your heart, Savannah.

Savannah had forgotten her grandmother's advice when she'd met Rob. She wasn't about to make the same mistake again.

"Come on. I'll show you the inside."

Savannah balked. "You're sure that your sister won't mind an extra houseguest?"

Carter glanced in the direction of the main house. The flash of some emotion—*guilt?*—didn't exactly put her mind at ease.

"Sergeant Wallace?"

"It's Carter, remember?" That elusive dimple made an appearance again. A secret weapon designed to sneak through a woman's defenses and affect her ability to think straight.

Fortunately, Savannah had become immune to a charming smile.

"Now that we've got that cleared up...how about answering my question?"

Chapter Five

Carter realized he'd made a tactical error. He should have known that Savannah would see through his pitiful attempt to sidestep the question before she unpacked her suitcase from the car.

"No one will mind a bit that you're here." Carter hoped it was true.

According to Maddie, the Colby family had taken Keira Wolfe in after she'd been injured in a car accident and suffered short-term memory loss. The veterinarian was now Jack's fiancé and staying in a guest room down the hall until the couple exchanged their vows. Violet also made room for Landon Derringer and Elise and her son, Cory, during their frequent visits to the ranch. Even in the midst of their own problems, it seemed that Violet and Jack didn't mind lending a helping hand to someone in need. And Savannah definitely qualified.

He couldn't help feeling protective of her. It wasn't that she appeared weak and helpless. Just the opposite. It couldn't be easy to accept help from strangers, and yet Savannah had done the best thing for her and the baby. He respected that. He respected *her*.

Relief took some of the starch out of Savannah's slender shoulders. "That's good, because I don't want to take advantage of your sister's hospitality."

Carter decided this might be a good time to clarify a few minor details. After all, Savannah would find them out sooner or later. Although if he had his way, later—*much* later—would be better.

"Maddie doesn't actually own the ranch," he admitted. "She's a…guest…here, too."

Savannah, who'd started up the narrow sidewalk, froze midstep. Twisted around to look at him.

"A guest?" she repeated.

"Belle Colby actually owns the Colby Ranch. Maddie is spending some time with Belle's… daughter."

Violet. Maddie's identical twin sister. His long lost *half* sister. Carter could barely make sense of what had happened, let alone try to explain it to someone else. And something told him this wasn't the time to launch into a lengthy explanation about the Wallace family tree. The one that had sprouted a few branches since his last deployment.

"So Belle Colby gave you permission to invite me here?" Savannah asked slowly.

Carter drove a hand through his hair. "Belle is… recovering from a riding accident that happened last summer. She's in a long-term care facility in Grasslands right now, but the family is…hopeful that she'll recover."

Savannah's lips parted but no sound came out. She glanced down at the keys clutched in her hand and Carter realized she was only seconds away from getting in the car and driving back to Dallas if he didn't explain.

"It's complicated." Really complicated.

Savannah's eyes narrowed. "What exactly is going on, Sergeant?" she demanded. "Are you dispensing information on a need-to-know basis only? Because if that's the case, I need to know a whole lot more before I accept your invitation to stay here."

Carter suppressed a smile. Savannah was downright beautiful when she got riled up. She got some color in her cheeks and those eyes…as green as cottonwood leaves.

"Fine. I'll try to explain. But keep in mind that sometimes truth is stranger than fiction—"

"There you are!"

Carter slowly turned around. Great. Just great. Walking toward them was the proof.

"Is that Maddie?" Savannah whispered.

Carter's eyes narrowed on the young woman striding toward them. Brown-and-gold-plaid shirt, complete with pearl buttons. A silver belt buckle roughly the size of a paperback novel.

And he still couldn't say for sure.

At some point over the past few months, Maddie had swapped her designer labels for Western wear. To make life even more interesting, the two women conspired together, taking an almost fiendish delight in making it difficult for people—like him—to figure out which one was which. Or who was who.

"Maybe."

"Maybe?" Savannah choked.

"I told you. It's—"

"Complicated?" A huff of frustration punctuated the sentence.

"Right."

"Darcy said she heard a car come up the driveway." The flip of a long copper ponytail provided the clue that Carter had been looking for.

Violet.

Once Maddie's hair got longer and she could copy her twin sister's hairstyle, he was going to be in big trouble.

"Now I know why you ran off before dessert." Violet gave him an I'll-deal-with-you-later look but smiled warmly at Savannah. "Who do we have here?"

Carter caught the brunt of Savannah's accusing gaze.

Okay. He already *was* in big trouble.

Knowing that Carter hadn't been completely honest left a bitter taste in Savannah's mouth.

She was going to have a few choice words with the man. But at the moment, Savannah had no idea what to say to the woman standing in front of her. The one whose eyes were bright with curiosity—and who obviously had no idea that Carter had invited a pregnant stranger to stay with them.

"This is Savannah Blackmore." Carter came to her rescue.

Nice of him, since he was the reason she was in this awkward predicament to begin with!

Good manners forced Savannah to clasp the hand the woman offered when what she really wanted to do was hide. "Hello."

"Savannah, Violet Colby—" For some reason, Carter stopped.

"Carter's sister." The woman nudged him aside and finished the introduction.

Savannah felt Carter stiffen beside her.

"You're Carter's…sister?"

And why hadn't he mentioned that when he'd talked about Maddie?

"When he wants to claim me." Violet smiled sweetly at her brother.

Carter shifted his weight, almost as if he were uncomfortable with the direction the conversation was going.

Well, good, Savannah thought. Why should she be the only one?

Savannah's gaze bounced back and forth between Carter and Violet Colby but she failed to find even the slightest resemblance between them. Carter was blond and blue-eyed while Violet's hair, as bright as a new penny, framed an oval face dominated by a pair of eyes the color of dark chocolate.

"Savannah lost her apartment a few days ago," Carter explained. "I was hoping it would be okay if she bunked in one of the cottages for a while."

"I'd like to rent it," Savannah interjected. "If that's all right with you."

Violet was already shaking her head. And even though Savannah had been ready to drive away a few minutes ago, the thought of leaving the Colby Ranch left her with a sudden, inexplicable chill.

"Renting is out of the question," Violet Colby said firmly. "We always make room for friends. And you and Carter are friends, right?"

Savannah didn't dare look at Carter. They weren't friends. She wasn't quite sure what they were.

"Savannah's husband, Rob, and I were stationed together in Afghanistan," Carter said quietly. "I promised him that I'd check on her when I came back to the States. Make sure she was doing all right. There was a misunderstanding with her lease and she needed a place to stay."

"Just for a few days," Savannah choked out, feeling the sting of Rob's betrayal all over again.

He'd asked Carter to check up on her?

Every letter she'd sent to Rob had been returned, unopened. At any time, he could have picked up the phone and called to find out how she was doing. But he hadn't. And then suddenly, it had been too late.

Savannah hadn't known there'd been another part to the promise Rob had held Carter to other than the one he'd delivered, but it explained why he'd offered her a place to stay. Left his number so she could get in touch with him if she changed her mind.

Violet's gaze dropped to Savannah's midsection for a split second before lifting again.

"You're more than welcome to move in for as long as you'd like." The genuine sincerity in her voice convinced Savannah more than the actual words. "My mom is one of those people who believes in sharing the blessings we've been given. She would want you to stay here. And so do I."

Savannah's grandmother had been the same way. Edith Callahan reached out to those in need whether they needed a hot meal or a hug. Or a place to stay. Savannah had witnessed it countless times, she'd just never expected to be the one on the receiving end.

"Thank you." Savannah felt tears sting the back of her eyes. "I…I don't mind helping out, either—"

"We agreed to talk about that later, didn't we?" Carter cut in.

"Was that an agreement?" Savannah tipped her head. "Because it sounded like an order to me."

"Well, I am a sergeant. So technically, I outrank you." Carter had the audacity to *wink* at her.

Savannah knew she should have been irritated by the outrageous statement. So why did she have to fight a sudden, overwhelming urge to smile?

A polite cough pulled her attention back to Violet. There was a speculative gleam in the chocolate-brown eyes; her expression disturbingly similar to the look Savannah had seen on Libby's face the day Carter had walked into the diner.

"Carter's right. We'll have plenty of time to talk about that later." Violet linked arms with her. "I'll show you the cottage and rustle up some fresh linens for the bed. If you don't think you'll be comfortable here, we can probably squeeze you in somewhere at the main house. But I have to warn you, there's a lot of hustle and bustle going on around the place."

Savannah didn't mention that she would welcome a little hustle and bustle. She'd lived a solitary life after her grandmother had passed away the previous year. The loneliness had briefly subsided during her whirlwind courtship with Rob, only to return with a vengeance when he'd left her a week after they'd exchanged vows.

Long days had slipped into sleepless nights. Until she'd found out that she was pregnant. An unexpected blessing but one that had turned her world upside down. Especially after any hope of reconciliation had ended with Rob's death.

Violet flipped on the porch light and pushed open the front door. "It's not very big," she warned. "But it's cozy."

Savannah felt tears sting the back of her eyes as she took in her surroundings.

The inside of the cottage was as quaint as the exterior. A pocket-size kitchen. Colorful rag rugs. Corduroy furniture with oversize cushions, as deep and inviting as feather pillows.

She'd dreamed of a place like this.

"Not quite what you expected, huh?"

Carter was suddenly standing beside her and Savannah realized he'd mistaken silence for disappointment.

"I didn't expect it to be—" She fumbled for the right description.

"So small?" Carter supplied.

Savannah shook her head.

"So...perfect."

"Perfect?" Carter's husky laugh rumbled out, wrapping around Savannah like one of the quilts that Violet was pulling out of the antique armoire in the corner.

"I know what you mean. I love the cottages, too." Violet shot him a quelling look. "But I love them even more when they're being used, so please, make yourself at home."

Savannah already felt at home. That was a problem she hadn't anticipated. She would accept the Colby's hospitality for one or two weeks. No longer. She would be gone by Thanksgiving. Gone before she grew too attached to the sunsets and fresh air and a blue sky that stretched for miles, giving her space to breathe.

Gone before Carter's smile had a chance to work its way into her heart.

Carter took a restless lap around the living room as Violet took charge. Compared to the apartment Savannah had been living in, he had to agree the cottage was an improvement.

"You should be warm enough tonight with a few extra blankets but I'll ask Jack to drop off a load of wood for the fireplace tomorrow. The weather around here can be as contrary as his favorite bull."

"Is Jack your husband?"

Violet's eyes widened in response to Savannah's innocent question. Which made him feel guilty. Carter didn't have to be an identical twin to know what Violet was thinking. If he and Savannah were close enough friends to warrant an invitation to stay at the ranch, wouldn't he have filled her in on some of his complicated family history?

"Older brother," she replied evenly. "Jack runs the cattle part of the Colby Ranch. I manage the truck farm and produce stand in town."

"I see," Savannah murmured.

Carter had no doubt about that whatsoever. Just like Violet, Savannah could see that he'd left out a few pertinent details when he'd invited her to stay at the ranch.

"I'll make up the bed while you unpack your things." Violet frowned and looked around. "Where is your suitcase?"

"It's still in the trunk of my car."

Violet looked at him now, eyebrow lifted, and Carter shook his head. No *way* he was leaving them alone. He didn't want to take the chance that Violet might accidentally ask Savannah questions that would open old wounds.

She ignored him—just like Maddie would have.

"Carter? Will you be a sweetheart and get Savannah's things while I find some fresh sheets for the bed?"

Carter had enlisted in the military five years ago, the ink barely dry on his high school diploma.

In spite of the sugarcoating on the words, he recognized a direct order when he heard one.

"Sure." He spun toward the door. It wasn't that he didn't trust Violet. He didn't *know* her.

But if she and Maddie were identical when it came to busybody tendencies, Carter figured he had better hurry.

Flecks of rust rained onto his boots when he lifted the trunk. Through a gaping hole in the metal, Carter could see the ground.

Rob had hinted that life had been good. He'd bragged about the house that he and Savannah planned to build, bordered by gardens because she loved flowers. Yellow roses, in particular.

So why was she driving an old beater with close to two-hundred-thousand miles on it?

There were a hundred questions Carter wanted to ask, but couldn't. Not yet. He'd seen the look on her face when Violet introduced herself. Savannah had assumed that he had lied to her. But the accusing look she'd tossed his way hadn't been the worst part. It was the look of resignation riding in its wake. As if she'd been *expecting* it.

Rob, what did you do?

And why had he thought that Carter could somehow make it right?

He grabbed Savannah's suitcase, a plaid relic as ancient as the car she drove, and made his way back to the cottage before Violet had a chance to interrogate Savannah about her personal life.

As his foot touched the top step, Violet's cheerful drawl stopped him in his tracks.

"So, how far along are you, Savannah?"

Carter winced.

Too late.

Chapter Six

"I'm back."

Carter lunged through the doorway and held up the suitcase, hoping to distract Violet.

She didn't so much as glance his way. Neither did Savannah.

Carter had been afraid this would happen. He dropped the suitcase with a thud. That didn't have the desired effect, either, although Violet did hold up one hand. Carter wasn't sure if she was acknowledging his presence or trying to shush him.

"You can put that in the bedroom, Carter."

Definitely the second one. Carter wondered if the bandana dangling from Violet's back pocket could be used as a muzzle.

Violet nodded at Savannah with a smile that encouraged her to continue.

"I'm six months along." The faintest hint of pink stained Savannah's cheeks.

Violet tipped her head. "So that means your baby is due sometime in February."

Savannah nodded. "The fourteenth."

"Really? Valentine's Day?" The woman who'd just tried to shush him released a piercing whistle, only several decibels lower than the one she used to summon her horse from the pasture. "That's awesome."

Carter silently did the math. Rob had been deployed the first week of June. The dates lined up with Savannah's claim that Rob had left her right before he enlisted.

The first time they'd met, his friend had bragged about his new wife. Her sweet personality. How beautiful she was.

But for some reason, Rob had neglected to mention that they'd been estranged before his death. Which meant that either his buddy's acting skills would have been worthy of an Academy Award—or Savannah was the one who wasn't being truthful about their relationship.

Neither possibility sat well with Carter.

"You must be pretty excited," Violet continued. "Do you know if you're having a boy or a girl?"

Carter cleared his throat. A less than subtle warning not to pry and one that Violet, of course, chose to ignore.

"I think—" Carter began. And then discovered that he couldn't. The simple ability to string several words together splintered under the impact of the smile that spread across Savannah's face.

Carter watched, mesmerized, as the woman in the photograph came to life right in front of his eyes. The sparkle in her eyes chased the shadows away until it looked as if she were lit from within.

"It's a girl," she said softly.

Violet reached down to plump one of the sofa cushions. "Do you have any names picked out?"

Carter opened his mouth. Closed it again. Not because he wanted to know if Savannah had any names picked out, but because she was *still* smiling. She didn't look uncomfortable or upset by Violet's questions. Questions that Carter hadn't thought to ask. Until this moment, he hadn't thought of the baby as being a separate person. A child who was going to grow up without knowing her father.

Because of him.

"Her name is Hope."

"Is that a family name?"

"No." Savannah settled one hand almost protectively on the rounded curve of her stomach. "It's a...reminder."

Something passed between her and Violet then. A look of understanding that told Carter the two women shared the same strong faith.

A few years ago, he wouldn't have felt like someone on the outside looking in. At the age of five, with Rachel's gentle guidance, Carter had knelt by his bed one night and prayed a child's simple prayer, asking Jesus to come into his heart. But somewhere along the way, life had become more complicated. Carter had witnessed people doing terrible things to each other—seen things that still haunted his dreams. He'd begun to think that God was as distant and unapproachable as his father.

Savannah had been through a lot the past few months and yet she hadn't turned her back on God. If she ever married again, it would be to a man whose faith was as solid as her own. A man who didn't have more questions than answers.

Married again?

Carter mentally slapped himself upside the head for even thinking along those lines. He'd provided Savannah with a place to stay. He planned to keep a discreet eye on her—from a distance. It was all he'd promised to do.

It was all he *could* do…

"I think Hope is a beautiful name. Don't you, Carter?"

Carter realized that Violet was talking to him now. He'd been distracted by the way the setting sun filtered through the curtains and picked out golden threads in Savannah's hair.

"Beautiful," he agreed absently.

Color flooded Savannah's cheeks and she averted her gaze.

Way to go, Wallace. Open mouth, insert combat boot.

Laughter danced in Violet's eyes. "I was talking about the name Savannah picked out for the baby. What were *you* talking about?"

"You and Maddie *are* alike," he muttered.

As if on cue, the front door swung open.

"Did someone say my name?"

Savannah's mouth dropped open as a young woman breezed into the cottage. A woman who, from the top of her shining copper hair to the silver tips on the toes of her cowboy boots, was the mirror image of Violet Colby.

"I thought I saw lights on over here. What's going on?" She parked her hands on her hips and looked around. Big brown eyes got even bigger when she spotted Savannah standing in the kitchen but she quickly recovered. "Hello."

Savannah glanced Carter's way, but he didn't seem inclined to rescue her this time. Call her crazy, but she got the distinct impression that *he* was the one who looked like he needed rescuing.

"Hi." Savannah scraped up a smile in response to the woman's cheerful greeting.

"This is Savannah," Violet interjected.

"Maddie Wallace."

So there really *was* a Maddie. Savannah supposed she should be grateful that Carter had told her the truth about that, even though he'd omitted a few other significant details about his family.

Like the fact that Maddie and Violet Colby were identical twins.

"Nice to meet you, Savannah." Maddie's smile grew and she turned to her sister. "I didn't realize we were expecting company this evening."

Carter didn't so much as blink, drat the man.

"That's all right." Savannah resisted the urge to cast a reproachful look in his direction. "Neither did Violet."

Maddie's forehead pleated, a sign of her confusion.

"Savannah is Carter's friend," Violet said helpfully. "She had some issues with her last apartment and needed a place to stay."

"Only for a few days." Savannah found herself repeating the words that were quickly becoming her theme song.

Violet pulled a set of bedsheets from another cabinet and the scent of lavender stirred the air. "I told her that we've got plenty of room."

"That's true enough." Maddie sauntered into the tiny living room. "Is there anything I can help with?"

"No, thanks. I think we're good," Violet told her twin.

Savannah cringed inwardly.

Although touched by their kindness, she didn't want Carter's sisters to feel like they had to fuss over her. Given the fact that Maddie and Violet hadn't known she was coming, they were handling her arrival with remarkable aplomb.

And neither one of them seemed to be in a hurry to leave.

Maddie reached for a stack of towels at the same time as Violet. They looked at each other and started to laugh.

In spite of her misgivings about Carter, Savannah couldn't help but be fascinated by the two women. She was an only child who had dreamed of having a large family someday, but to have an identical twin sister? She couldn't imagine what that would be like....

"Weird, isn't it?" Maddie grinned.

Savannah felt her cheeks heat up. "I'm sorry. I didn't mean to stare."

"That's okay." Violet gave Savannah's arm a friendly pat. "Most of the time, Carter can't tell us apart, either."

Shaking his head, Carter grumbled, "It might help if you didn't *dress* alike."

Maddie hooked her thumbs in the front pockets of her jeans and stuck out a foot. "Maybe it's the boots," she mused.

"Or the matching belt buckles?" Carter said under his breath.

"Well, it certainly can't be the Texas drawl." Maddie looked smug. "I've been practicing, *y'all*."

Carter rolled his eyes.

"That's right. You'll be speaking fluent cowgirl in no time," Violet teased.

Maddie turned to Savannah. "Where are you from?"

Carter shifted his stance, a movement that blocked Maddie from her view. Savannah got the distinct impression it wasn't an accident.

"I think we should leave Savannah alone so she can settle in. She's probably tired from the long drive." Carter's voice sounded strange. Almost as if he were gritting his teeth.

"You're right." Maddie peeked around his shoulder and smiled at Savannah. "How long of a drive *was* it?"

"I live in Dallas."

Carter cleared his throat.

"Catching a cold, little brother?" Maddie patted his arm.

"Lupita has a special remedy that will fix you up." Violet flashed an impish look. "But don't worry, it tastes better than it smells."

Maddie and Violet snickered. In harmony.

Savannah decided that she liked Carter's sisters already.

"Is that where you and Carter met? In Dallas?"

Savannah nodded, wondering why Carter seemed tense. It wasn't as if the questions she was being asked were difficult—

"How long have you two known each other?"

Except for that one.

Savannah swallowed hard, unsure of how to answer the question. What would Carter's sisters think of her if she told them that she'd met him less than a week ago? Would they think she was taking advantage of their hospitality?

"Not very long—"

"For a while."

Savannah's statement collided with Carter's in midair, leaving her momentarily speechless.

How could Carter stand there and tell his sisters something that wasn't true?

Two pairs of matching brown eyes bounced back and forth between her and Carter.

Now that the two women stood side by side, Savannah could see subtle differences between the two. Violet's complexion tinted bronze from the sun, evidence of hours spent outdoors. And Maddie's auburn hair was an inch or two shorter than her sister's....

Savannah groaned when she saw Maddie grin at her twin. "I'm doing it again, aren't I?"

"Don't worry. Violet and I are still getting used to it," Violet said.

"Getting used to what?" Savannah asked curiously.

"Seeing each other. I mean, we met five months ago, but it's weird to see your face on someone else."

Savannah tried to hide her confusion. And her rising frustration with the one person in the room who'd only said that his family situation was *complicated.*

Violet looked at Maddie. Who looked at her brother.

They folded their arms.

"You didn't tell her."

Carter had never seen a simple mission go south quite the way this one had.

"I thought she might want to wait for the movie."

"Ignore my brother, Savannah," Maddie huffed. "He has a warped sense of humor."

Carter gave her a look. "It certainly helps in this family."

"Violet and I met for the first time last summer," Maddie explained. "She *accidentally* found me. After Landon found her, that is."

"We were pretty shocked," her sister added.

Shocked wasn't exactly the word Carter would have chosen.

"You didn't grow up together?" Savannah pressed her hand against her lips the moment the words slipped out.

"Neither of us knew the other one existed. I grew up on the ranch and she grew up in the city, but we're hoping it didn't cause irreversible damage."

Carter knew Violet was teasing, her own attempt to lighten the moment, but the words hit too close to home. Whatever the circumstances had been that caused Belle and his father to part ways, they wouldn't be able to undo the damage they'd inflicted on their children. Maddie and Violet. Gray and Jack. None of them could recover the years they'd lost.

Something must have shown in his expression, because Maddie looked at Violet and shook her head.

"It's a long story," she murmured. "I'm sure Carter will explain everything when he has some time."

Savannah glanced at him, and Carter saw the doubt shimmering in her eyes. He'd had the time, when she questioned him on the way to the cottage.

Savannah grasped the back of a chair with both

hands, a weary gesture that brought him to her side in an instant.

"Are you all right?"

Savannah's teeth sank into her lower lip. "A little tired, I guess."

"That's it. We're out of here." Violet gave the afghan draped over the back of the sofa a final pat.

"Is there anything else you need before you turn in for the night?" Maddie asked.

"I'll be fine. Really."

Savannah's smile was convincing. Almost.

"We'll see you in the morning, then. Lupita is making her famous buttermilk pancakes." Violet tossed a smile over her shoulder as she walked with Maddie to the door. "If you need anything, just give a holler."

Finally.

Carter tried to conceal his relief. Once Maddie and Violet were out of the way, he could do damage control. Although he couldn't shake the sneaking suspicion that he'd been the one responsible for the damage in the first place.

His plan was thwarted when Maddie reached out and grabbed his hand.

"You're coming with us, Carter. Violet and I need your help with something, too."

Before Carter could protest, Violet had taken hold of his other hand.

"Two against one?" he muttered.

He thought he heard someone laugh. But when he looked over his shoulder, Savannah was already disappearing into the bedroom.

"You better get used to it." Maddie smiled sweetly.

Carter, who knew a dozen ways to extricate himself from a difficult situation, found himself being herded out of the cottage and up the driveway like one of Jack's stray calves.

Chapter Seven

Carter saw a light on in the kitchen and hoped it was Gray. His brother would recognize a hostage situation and intervene. After all, the guy *was* a professional.

Unfortunately, it was Keira, Jack's fiancée, who sat at the table, hands cradling a steaming cup of tea, a stethoscope still draped around her neck.

No help there. One of Maddie and Violet's allies, not his.

"Hey, ya'll." The veterinarian looked up as they shuffled past the doorway, Maddie and Violet attached to his side like a pair of amateur country line dancers. "Care to join me?"

"Sure," Violet sang out.

Maddie bobbed her head. "We'll be right back. We have to talk to Carter for a minute."

Talk?

Carter wasn't fooled by Maddie's bright smile. He was being hauled in for questioning.

"Aren't I entitled to a phone call?" he quipped.

"No."

Carter winced when the emphatic retort rang in both his ears at the exact same moment.

"My favorite meal?"

"Move it, soldier."

Violet kicked the door shut in some cowgirl-ninja move that left Carter inwardly shaking his head. Then he was free.

Sort of.

"Okay, let's hear it." They folded their arms, stared him down.

Carter felt like he was back in boot camp, under the gimlet eye of his commanding officer and resisted a crazy urge to salute.

"Everything," Violet said promptly.

"And don't even bother to waste our time with that name, rank and serial-number stuff," Maddie warned. "You know what she means."

Carter checked a smile. "You've been watching too many old movies."

"And you're stalling." Maddie's chin hiked up a notch. "Why didn't you tell us you invited Savannah to the ranch?"

"Because the first time I asked her, she turned me down." Flat. "I didn't think she would change her mind."

Maddie and Violet exchanged a look.

"That's why you moved into Gray's room instead of taking the cottage Violet offered," Maddie said slowly. "You were *hoping* that she would."

He couldn't argue with that, either. "Savannah didn't have anywhere else to go. She planned to stay in a hotel while she looked for another apartment."

Maddie continued to study him and Carter could almost see the wheels turning in her head.

"When we were at Gray's apartment the day you got back, you mentioned there was someone you had to see before you came to the ranch. Was it Savannah?"

Maybe Maddie should have been the detective in the family.

"Yes."

"You've never mentioned her before. How do you two know each other?"

Carter felt a hitch in his breathing.

"Her husband, Rob—" He managed to push the name out, past the lump that instantly formed in his throat. "He asked me to check on Savannah when I got back to the States."

"Then I'd say it's a good thing you did. Will he be home for Thanksgiving?"

Violet's innocent question landed like a punch to the gut. Pain radiated through his body, leaving Carter unable to do anything but shake his head.

He hadn't talked to his siblings about what happened to Rob. How did you put something like that in an email? Every time he said Rob's name, it was ripping the bandage from a fresh wound.

For the first time since he'd come home, Carter understood why Maddie and Gray had waited to share the news of their father's disappearance in person.

"You wrote that one of your friends was killed," Maddie whispered. "Were you talking about Savannah's husband?"

"He died in a roadside bombing two months ago." In Carter's arms.

The color drained from Violet's face. "Savannah must be devastated."

"And she's expecting." Maddie briefly closed her eyes. "I can't imagine what she's going through. Knowing that her husband will never have the chance to hold his child."

The child he hadn't known about.

The thought never made it past Carter's lips. Better to let them think that everything between Rob and Savannah had been fine. Until a week ago, it was what he'd believed, too.

Accepting the alternative was the equivalent of accepting Rob's death all over again…and he wasn't ready to do that. Not yet.

"Does she have any family?"

Carter had wondered the same thing. He'd tried

to recall if Rob had mentioned anything about parents. Siblings. "I'm not sure. I don't think so."

"Well, she has us now," Violet said. "I meant what I said when I told Savannah that she is welcome to stay as long as she'd like."

"Thank you." Carter meant it, but suddenly it didn't seem like enough. "And I'm sorry I overstepped my bounds. I should have asked your permission to invite Savannah to the ranch."

Violet acknowledged the statement with a jerky nod, pivoting toward the door as if she couldn't get away from him fast enough now.

"Violet?"

She stopped and reluctantly turned to face him.

"Is something else bothering you?" Carter asked cautiously.

"Yes." Hurt flashed in Violet's eyes. "Your apology."

Apparently he'd somehow messed that up, too. "This is your home and I had no right to invite someone to stay here without asking your permission first—"

"Stop right there."

Carter stopped.

"You don't *have* to apologize at all."

"I don't?"

"I want you to think of the ranch as your home."

Violet's chin lifted and she looked him straight in the eye. "And do you know why?"

She didn't wait for him to answer.

"Because like it or not, Carter, *I'm* your sister, too."

The door closed softly behind her.

A peaceful silence settled into the corners of the room as Savannah started to unpack her things into a stout antique dresser next to the bed.

The faint scent of lavender from a sachet tucked in the corner stirred the air, soothed the raw edges of her emotions. Already she could feel her heart settling into the beauty of her surroundings.

Framed in the weathered window frame, a star winked against the indigo sky. A sky the same shade of blue as Carter's eyes....

Savannah yanked the unruly thought back in line.

She didn't want to think about Carter. And she certainly didn't want to notice the man's eyes.

Or the emotion she'd seen lingering there, one Savannah recognized all too well in spite of his attempt to hide it.

Pain.

The comment he'd made about his family situation being complicated made sense in light of what she'd just found out.

Identical twins, separated. Why?

Savannah felt a delicate flutter below her rib cage

and the rush of love that inevitably followed in its wake. She would do anything to protect her child.

Maybe Carter's parents had felt the same way. Had circumstances forced them to separate their daughters?

The deep affection between Violet and Maddie appeared genuine. Real. But judging from some of the comments Carter had made in the car, he didn't think of the Colby ranch as home. He'd claimed Maddie as his sister, but not Violet. And if Jack Colby was Violet's older brother, didn't that mean he was Carter's brother, too?

Savannah was beginning to believe that Carter hadn't been exaggerating when he'd described his family situation as "complicated."

But where did he fit in the equation…and in the family?

Not that it was any of her business. Carter had provided Savannah with a place to stay, not given her access to his personal life.

She had her own secrets to keep. Things that Carter wouldn't want to know, considering that he and Rob had been friends.

The less time she spent in his company, the better. Carter Wallace was too observant, attuned to the slightest change in her expression the way he would notice a shift in the wind. Savannah didn't need—or want—that kind of attention. It could only lead to trouble.

He was a soldier. Hardwired to defend. Protect. It would be too easy to rest her head on that broad shoulder. Seek shelter and safety in his arms.

She'd trusted Rob and look what had happened. Now she was determined to make a new start for her and the baby.

Savannah smoothed out a wrinkle in the quilt and straightened one of the decorative pillows, a square of faded pink muslin with a verse from the Bible neatly embroidered inside the hedge of delicate ruffles.

Rejoice always. Pray without ceasing. In everything give thanks.

Her grandmother would have approved, especially the giving thanks part. She could still hear Edith Callahan's lilting voice.

Count to ten, Savannah. Count to ten.

As always, her grandmother had put her own unique spin on the familiar advice. It hadn't been a reminder to hold her tongue or her temper. Her grandmother encouraged Savannah to count her blessings—and not to stop until she got to ten.

Savannah had embraced the words. In elementary school, when she struggled to fit in at her new school after her parents had divorced and left her in the care of her elderly grandmother because neither of them wanted their daughter along the journey to find themselves. During her senior year of high school, when Edith's health started to decline following a stroke that put Savannah in charge of the tiny household. The last few months of Edith's life, when Savannah dropped out of college to take care of her.

There were times in Savannah's life when she'd flown past ten and kept right on going—and times when it took every ounce of strength to reach that particular number.

Like the day Rob had told her that their marriage had been a mistake. The day he'd walked out the door without looking back.

Savannah closed her eyes. Shut out the memories of the past that threatened to drag her down again. Focused on the present.

Tonight it wasn't difficult at all to find things to be thankful for. Her car hadn't broken down on the way to Grasslands. A place to stay. Space to think. Room to breathe. Violet. Maddie...

Savannah stopped, afraid to add the name that hovered at the edges of the prayer. It didn't matter. He appeared in her thoughts, anyway.

The man whose smile threatened to sneak through her defenses when she'd promised herself she would never let her guard down again.

Carter stood on the front porch of the cottage, wondering if he should take his own advice and let Savannah have the rest of the evening to settle in. Alone.

Except that he wanted to be sure her suitcase hadn't found its way back to the trunk of her car again. The way she'd grabbed on to the chair for support continued to bother him, too. Savannah had claimed she was tired—but Carter couldn't shake the feeling there was more to it than that.

He knocked once, lightly, just in case she'd already fallen asleep.

The light flicked on above Carter's head, dousing him with a spray of light. The door opened a crack and a pair of spring green eyes met his.

Carter lifted up the plate of leftovers he'd commandeered from the fridge.

"I thought you might be hungry."

The door opened a little wider and Savannah reached for the plate. A mouthwatering aroma drifted from the foil-covered dish.

"This smells wonderful."

A low rumble of appreciative agreement followed the statement and Savannah pressed one hand against her stomach, clearly mortified.

"I believe that's the typical response to Lupita's cooking." Carter couldn't help but grin. And he took full advantage of the moment and ducked inside the cottage, taking a brief but thorough inventory on his way to the kitchen.

Relief poured through him.

Not a suitcase in sight.

"You didn't have to do this, you know." Savannah followed, a look of consternation on her pretty face.

"I wasn't sure if you'd stopped for something to eat along the way."

The telltale color that bloomed in her cheeks told Carter his hunch had been right.

"I had some fruit," she murmured.

"If you write down a list of your favorite foods, I'm sure Lupita will add them to the cart the next time she goes shopping."

Savannah looked almost horrified by the suggestion. Not quite the reaction Carter had anticipated.

"I can drive to the grocery store in Grasslands," she protested. "I don't expect special treatment. Just…pretend I'm not here."

Somehow, Carter doubted that was possible. He hadn't been able to stop thinking about Savannah since the day they'd met.

But she'd been wary of his motives then and judging from the expression on her face, those feelings hadn't changed.

Maddie and Violet were right.

He had some explaining to do.

"Thank you for bringing over dinner." Savannah set the plate down on the table and summoned a polite smile.

Carter's cue to leave. Which he ignored.

"Aren't you going to eat?"

"Yes." And then a cautious, "Are you going to stay?"

"Don't mind if I do."

Carter heard a faint but unmistakable chirp of alarm as he pulled a chair away from the table and guided Savannah into it.

He ignored that, too.

"Let's see what we've got here." Carter peeled the foil off the tray even though he already knew what was underneath it. "Baby red potatoes. Cloverleaf rolls. Sweet potato pie. Fried chicken. Ah, and my favorite Texas staple—barbecued ribs."

Savannah stared down at the variety of food mounded together on the platter. Carter didn't know what she liked, so he'd added a little of everything he'd discovered in the refrigerator. A veritable culinary relief map of texture and color.

"Is that a…waffle?" Savannah was pointing to something next to the green beans.

"Uh-huh. There are also bagels and cream cheese if you want to sleep in tomorrow morning and skip breakfast at the main house," Carter added casually.

Savannah's eyes narrowed.

"You wouldn't be trying to keep me away from your family, would you?"

Carter didn't miss a beat.

"Yes, ma'am."

Chapter Eight

"Carter—" Savannah's gurgle of laughter took them both by surprise.

They stared at each other across the table, a fragile silence humming between them, linking them together.

Carter pushed to his feet. The chair scraped against the floor and shattered the moment.

"Better dig in before it gets cold," he said, struggling to regain his equilibrium. "I'll see if there's anything to drink."

He retrieved a bottle of water from the fridge and shut the door just in time to see Savannah bow her head and close her eyes.

Carter felt a strange tightening in his chest as a silky tassel of toffee-colored hair slid forward, outlining the delicate curve of her jaw.

His fingers twitched with the urge to smooth it

away from her face. To trace the half smile that touched her lips as her lips moved in silent petition.

A moment later Savannah's head lifted and she looked across the table at him, the smile still there, in her eyes.

"What did you pray for?" Carter couldn't prevent the words from slipping out.

"That I would continue to seek God's guidance," she said softly.

Something Carter had stopped asking long ago.

"And—" Savannah hesitated, stirring his curiosity in spite of the fact that talking about God left Carter feeling uncomfortable. Restless.

Envious.

"And—?" he prompted.

To Carter's absolute amazement, Savannah blushed.

And you.

Savannah wondered what Carter would say if she said the words out loud.

She hadn't meant to pray for him. By all rights, she should still be upset with him.

She *was* still upset with him.

He hadn't even bothered to tell his sisters that he'd offered her one of the cottages, making for an awkward first meeting....

"Yeah, I'm sorry about that."

Savannah blinked, wondering if she'd said the

words out loud. Because it was unsettling to think that Carter could read her mind.

"I should have told Violet that I'd invited you to stay here."

Yes, he should have. He should have told her *a lot* of things. Savannah flattened a piece of potato with the back of her fork.

"Ouch."

Savannah glanced up and her heart got tangled in Carter's rueful smile.

"I'm glad you're taking out your frustration on those poor vegetables instead of me."

"I'm not—" Savannah started to deny it, but the proof was there, soaking in a pool of barbecue sauce.

A wave of fatigue swept in, eroding what remained of her energy.

"I don't know how to do this, either."

Savannah's gaze lifted to Carter. "Do what?"

"This." He leaned back in the chair and studied her. Serious. Intent. One hundred percent soldier. "Trying to figure out what to say. What not to say. How *much* to say."

For some reason, the candid admission moved Savannah more than the smile.

She traced a vine embroidered on the tablecloth. "Neither do I."

Savannah didn't know if she could trust him. Wasn't sure she could trust herself anymore.

"Did you ever play the game twenty questions when you were a kid?"

It was the last thing Savannah expected Carter to say.

"Yes," she said cautiously.

"Good. You start. We each get one question."

"I thought it was twenty questions."

"It's late—I'm fast-tracking this." Carter's lips curled at the edges. "You can ask another one tomorrow."

She would never have guessed that the man would have a whimsical bone in his body. His attempt to lighten the moment, put her at ease was charming...and terrifying.

Savannah speared a piece of chicken with her fork, thinking hard. Afraid to delve too deeply into his personal life because he might expect her to do the same.

Some of the names Savannah heard mentioned scrolled through her mind.

Jack Colby. Landon.

Or did she ask about Maddie and Violet, who claimed to have met only five months ago?

Carter's fingers drummed against the edge of the table and he lifted an eyebrow.

Savannah took the hint.

"The woman you said was injured in a riding accident. Belle Colby? Who is she?"

Carter's expression darkened and Savannah immediately wished she could take it back.

"I'm sorry—"

"No, it's a fair question," he interrupted. "You just happened to pick the one question no one knows the answer to." The chair creaked as Carter shifted his weight. "We do know that Belle Colby is Maddie and Violet's biological mother."

But not Carter's, she guessed.

"Maddie and Gray—he's the oldest in my family—grew up thinking that Sharla Wallace was our mother. Our dad never said anything that led us to believe she hadn't given birth to all three of us. Not even after she died in a car accident when I was three."

"I'm so sorry." Savannah found herself mouthing the words that had brought little comfort when she'd learned of Rob's death.

"I don't remember her." The words were spoken matter-of-factly, but the flash of pain in Carter's eyes spoke of a wound that had never completely healed.

"A few months ago, after Belle's accident, Violet went on a search for her biological father in Fort Worth. She found Maddie instead. It turns out that my dad had been married to Belle Colby. No one knows why they divorced."

The edge of bitterness in Carter's voice cut deep; his eyes flashed a silent warning to keep her distance. Savannah laced her fingers together in her lap because her first inclination was to reach for his hand.

To let him know that she understood what it was like to have your world turned upside down in the blink of an eye. To discover that all the things you'd thought were real had been based on secrets. Lies. But even more difficult to accept when they came from someone you loved.

"A few months ago, Violet's fiancé, Landon Derringer, hired a private investigator to do some digging into Belle's past. He hit a brick wall. There *is* no Belle Colby. Technically, the woman doesn't exist. At some point she took on a new identity. Gray's a cop and he's been using his connections to piece everything together, but so far, he's come up empty-handed."

Savannah tried to come up with reasons why a woman with young children would change her name. Cloak herself in secrecy. None of them were good.

"Even if your parents divorced, your dad must know something," she ventured.

"He might, but no one has been able to question him," Carter said tightly. "Dad's a medical missionary and he went off the grid near the Mexican border last summer. None of us has been able to get in touch with him. As far as I know, he doesn't even realize I'm back in the States. Not that it would have made a difference," he added. "It's not like he put aside his work the last time I was home on leave."

"It must have been difficult, to be so far away when you found out," Savannah said softly.

"I wasn't that far away," Carter said wryly. "Maddie and Gray decided it would be better to tell me in person. I found out about an hour after I stepped off the plane last Saturday."

The day before they'd met.

Savannah pulled in a breath so sharp it felt like a knife sliding between her ribs. Carter had been dealing with all of this and yet he'd sought her out at the diner, to deliver Rob's message.

It revealed the kind of man he was. A man who set aside his feelings to do the right thing.

"The police must be involved if your father is missing."

"He's not considered missing. That's part of the problem. If we had proof of foul play, the authorities would get involved, but unfortunately, this is Dad's MO. He gets completely focused on his work and forgets everything else."

Including his children, Savannah thought.

"He's supposed to be back for Thanksgiving," Carter continued. "That's why Maddie insisted that I stick around for a few weeks. Once he plugs into the outside world again, he'll know we're here, at the ranch, waiting."

"Praying," Savannah murmured.

"I'll leave that to the rest of the family." Bitterness edged into Carter's voice. "No matter what Dad says, nothing will be the same. I mean, maybe we'll finally understand why he and Belle split up, but nothing they say can ever make up for the damage they caused by splitting up two sets of twins."

There was no way—*no way*—Savannah had heard that correctly.

"You mean Violet and Maddie."

"And Gray and Jack Colby. They're identical twins, too."

Carter waited for the gasp of surprise. The expression of disbelief.

Instead, he was blindsided by Savannah's wistful smile.

"You're so lucky."

"Lucky?"

"No, not lucky," Savannah corrected. *Now* she was making some sense. Until she added, "Blessed. To have family. People who…want to be with you."

Carter hadn't considered that. Sure, Violet and Jack were okay but they were Maddie and Gray's identical twins. It was difficult to wrap his mind around the fact that they were his family, too, no matter what Violet had said in the den a little while ago.

"They're my *half* siblings. And Gray—" Carter couldn't even say it out loud. He still couldn't accept that a guy named Joe Earl could be Gray's father, not even if Joe's own wife believed it. Patty Earl had hinted that Belle Colby, at the age of sixteen, had been more attracted to the inheritance Brian Wallace would eventually receive from his grandmother than she was to Joe.

Violet was adamant that her mother wouldn't have married Carter's father for money. It was a touchy subject—one that Maddie had warned him not to bring up when Violet or Jack were around.

People in a small town talked and Belle's reputation had already come under suspicion when James Crawford, the original owner of the spread, had left the ranch to her after he died.

Belle had become a wealthy woman over the years, something that might have prompted Patty Earl's decision to get to know "her" boys.

The thought sickened Carter. It was one thing to maintain a polite distance from Jack Colby, but what would it do to his relationship with Gray if they discovered the only thing they had in common was the fact they'd been lied to all these years?

"What about Gray?"

Compassion shimmered in Savannah's eyes and

Carter mentally took a step back. He hadn't meant to go into so much detail. He'd invited her to stay at the Colby Ranch in an attempt to ease her burden, not add to it.

"You only get one question, remember? You can ask another one tomorrow. Now it's my turn."

Savannah's fork clattered onto the plate.

It was clear she assumed that he was going to question her about Rob. What had gone wrong in their marriage? Why he'd left her?

Questions that Carter wanted the answers to—but not if they brought that wary look back into Savannah's eyes.

Maybe someday she would trust him.

Savannah's teeth sank into her lower lip but she lifted her chin to meet his gaze.

"What do you want to know?"

Carter leaned forward, elbows propped on the table.

Smiled.

"Are you going to eat that waffle?"

Chapter Nine

"Got a minute?"

Carter took one look at his brother's serious expression and *knew* he should have gone straight to his room instead of taking a detour to the study to check his email.

The conversation with Savannah had left him feeling restless, the words she'd said continuing to play through his mind.

You're so blessed to have family.

Whenever Carter had thought through every scenario, he'd always thought of the outcome in terms of what he could lose, never what he might gain.

Carter shut down the computer so Gray wouldn't see what he'd been up to.

"I was just keeping up with traffic, officer."

"I'm off duty." Gray's lips twitched. "And from what I heard, you already got busted."

"Twice. Or—" Carter tipped his head thoughtfully "—maybe it only counts as once if the women who chewed you out are identical twins?"

"I'll have to look that one up in the statutes." Gray sauntered into the room and pulled up a chair.

Uh-oh.

"Are you sure I don't need a lawyer?"

Carter was only half joking.

"Maddie said you invited a friend to stay at the ranch for a while."

This was about *Savannah?*

Carter immediately bristled. "Is that a problem?"

Gray leaned forward and met his gaze.

"You tell me."

Carter wasn't fooled by the mild response.

"Let me guess. You want her full name and date of birth?"

"Do you know them?"

Carter ignored the question. "Savannah was being evicted from her apartment."

"And she didn't have anywhere else to go?"

The flash of skepticism in Gray's eyes turned up the heat under Carter's temper. "No."

"And you're sure...Savannah...isn't taking advantage of the situation?"

"Moving to the ranch was a last resort. She didn't want to come here." Not only that, Carter had a feeling that Savannah was already working on an exit plan. She'd made it clear she didn't want to be a burden.

"I'm surprised you never mentioned her, that's all."

"You're surprised," Carter repeated. "Really? Because we haven't exactly exchanged diaries over the past few years."

"You keep a diary?"

"You're worse than Maddie," Carter scoffed.

"And you're avoiding the question."

"I didn't realize you'd asked one."

Gray's bark of laughter echoed around the room, defusing the tension in the air. "Sorry. Elise says that sometimes I use that voice on her, too. I sounded like a cop just now, didn't I?"

He sounded like a big brother. Carter wasn't sure quite what to do with that. The changes in their family structure hadn't been the only ones he'd noticed in Gray since he'd arrived at the Colby Ranch. There'd been a few changes on the *inside,* too.

"Savannah isn't going to take advantage of Violet's hospitality. Or steal the silver," he added.

A heartbeat of silence followed.

"After dealing with Patty Earl, I admit I'm a little suspicious of people's motives," Gray finally admitted. "Jack and I suspect the only reason she's been trying to cozy up to us is because she found out the Colby Ranch is a lucrative operation."

Carter didn't want to be reminded of the woman who'd claimed that her husband was Jack and Gray's biological father.

Another secret. One that could have led to his father and Belle Colby's breakup. But if Gray and Jack weren't Brian's sons, why hadn't both boys stayed with Belle?

If these were the questions that Gray had been wrestling with the past few months, no wonder he was tense.

Carter released a slow breath, reminding himself to cut the guy some slack.

"I promised my friend Rob that I would check on Savannah. Make sure she was okay. I'm guessing that meant he didn't want her living on the street."

Instead of taking offense, Gray regarded him thoughtfully, leaving Carter to wonder what else Maddie and Violet had told him.

"You remind me of Dad."

Carter stiffened. "Sorry."

"It was a compliment, Carter. Dad has devoted most of his life to taking care of people. Making sure they were okay."

Carter couldn't argue with that, but it would have been nice if their father had spent some time with his own family, too. Instead, he'd left them in Rachel's care.

Gray nodded, almost as if he'd read Carter's thoughts. "I always wondered why Dad seemed to think that his patients needed him, but it never seemed to cross his mind that we did, too."

Carter tried not to show how stunned he was by the quiet admission.

He had never considered the possibility that Gray might have felt the same way he did. Guilty for wanting their father's attention. But tossing a football in the backyard had seemed a frivolous thing compared to treating people who were injured. Sick. People who needed Brian Wallace more.

"Dad always told us to trust God—but it would have been nice if he would have trusted us, too." Carter couldn't keep the edge of bitterness from his voice.

"You're talking about Belle."

"Dad shouldn't have kept something like that a secret. Aren't you angry that he kept you from knowing your twin brother all these years?"

"We can't change the past," Gray said evenly. "All we can do, with God's help, is move forward."

"Easier said than done."

"It's occurred to me that Dad might have kept his distance from us for a reason," Gray went on. "No one knows why he and Belle split up—or why they split *us* up—but it must have been pretty big. Maybe his work is his way of trying to make up for something. Something he considered a… personal failure."

Carter wandered over to the window overlooking the courtyard to hide his expression.

He had more in common with his dad than Gray thought.

"For what it's worth, Violet and Maddie agreed that Savannah should stay here, too." His brother rose to his feet. "I guess the majority rules on this one."

"She needs some time."

"Meaning?"

"Meaning you don't get to interrogate her, Office Wallace."

A smile played at the corner of Gray's lips. "Got it. I'll see you in the morning. I'm sticking around until Sunday night."

"Thanks for the warning."

"It's better than a ticket," Gray quipped.

Carter's eyes narrowed. "I don't remember you having a sense of humor."

"You can thank Elise for that, too. The love of a good woman…" Gray began to whistle as he sauntered out the door.

Carter couldn't remember his brother ever whistling, either.

The love of a good woman…

Unbidden, an image of Savannah's face flashed through his mind.

No way. Not going there.

Carter wandered back to the desk and faced the computer again. Belle Colby smiled at him from inside a metal picture frame beside the monitor. Carter couldn't help but stare at the woman who didn't even know she'd turned his life—and several others—upside down. It was a candid shot, taken while Belle was sitting on a hay bale. Ribbons of sunlight winnowed through the cracks in the barn board, illuminating a face that was both familiar and strange at the same time.

Shoulder-length auburn hair. Wide, sparkling brown eyes. The strong resemblance between her and Maddie was almost eerie, but that wasn't what Carter found the most unsettling.

Who *was* she? Had his dad loved Belle? Had he married Sharla to provide his children with a mother or because he'd fallen in love with her?

Where are you, Dad? We need some answers.

Carter opened up his email account and skimmed through the messages in the in-box.

Nothing new.

Almost of their own volition, his fingers began tapping out a message.

Maddie and Violet said that every letter they'd

sent to their father had been ignored, but something pushed Carter to try again.

Dear Dad,
When you get this message, please call me. I'm back from Afghanistan now and staying at the Colby Ranch in Grasslands with Gray and Maddie. We're all worried because we haven't heard from you in a while. Can you take a few minutes to let us know you're okay? There are some things going on that you should know about....

Things he needed to know.

Carter hesitated, unsure how to end it.

He released a slow breath. Wrote his name. Hit Send.

A few seconds later, a new message appeared. Carter's heart buckled.

Message returned. Unable to deliver.

He pushed to his feet, palms flat against the desk. Holding him upright because he didn't trust his knees to do their job.

What had he expected?

Without realizing it, Carter reached for the Bible that lay open on the desk, traced the embossed letters on the cover with the tip of his finger. While he was growing up, Rachel had encouraged him to read a passage every day.

It's a love letter from God, Carter.

A letter he hadn't read for a long time. And right now, God was silent. And as unreachable as his father.

Pressing a hand against the small of her back, Savannah eased into one of the chairs on the porch. In the distance she could see the boxy silhouettes of the Herefords grazing on a hill in the distance. Hear a low whicker from the horses in the corral and the rumble of a utility vehicle.

She hadn't seen anyone since Violet had delivered a basket of warm muffins and a container of fresh fruit right to her door that morning.

Savannah felt a stab of guilt that she'd let Carter's sister think she'd missed breakfast because she'd slept in. The truth was, she'd been avoiding Carter.

It was only a matter of time before he asked the questions she had seen simmering in his eyes the night before.

Questions about Rob.

What was she supposed to say? That the man Carter obviously respected and admired had walked out a week after he'd promised to love and cherish her forever?

Carter hadn't been able to conceal his bitterness over the secrets his father had kept from the family. How would he react if he ever learned the whole truth about Rob?

A flurry of movement caught her eye and someone ducked behind one of the shrubs that formed a hedge between the two cottages.

A very small someone.

Savannah angled her head, trying to get a better look.

"Hello?"

A pair of big brown eyes peeked over the leaves. "Hi."

Savannah lifted one hand and motioned her over. "You can come over, if you'd like."

"I don't want to disturb you."

"You aren't disturbing me. I promise."

There was a rustling sound and a little girl about seven or eight years old inched into view. She wore a denim skirt with an embroidered ruffle around the bottom and a matching vest. Tiny cowboy boots completed the adorable ensemble.

Carter hadn't been kidding when he'd said there were a lot of people coming and going at the ranch. Was she the daughter of the housekeeper? One of the ranch hands?

"I'm Savannah."

"I know that." The child giggled.

Savannah realized that word of her arrival must have gotten out. "And you are—"

"Darcy Garland."

"Do you live around here, Darcy?"

"The white house with the green door." Darcy pointed farther down the row of cottages. "My daddy is the foreman. That means he's the boss," she added proudly.

"I see." Savannah tucked away a smile. "I haven't had a chance to meet him yet. I just got here last night."

"I haven't lived here very long, either," Darcy said. "But you'll like it. I do. It's the best place in the world. I know where all the good hiding spots are." Her voice dropped to a whisper. "And where Lupita keeps the extra cookies."

"Lupita is the cook," Savannah remembered.

"Uh-huh. And she scolds people if they forget to take off their boots."

The cook and the housekeeper. Any ideas Savannah had entertained about helping out around the house died a quick death.

Savannah patted the wicker chair next to hers. "You're welcome to join me, if you'd like."

"Can't." Darcy wagged her head from side to side, setting the glossy brown ponytail swinging like a pendulum. "Uncle Carter said that no one's s'posed to bother you."

"Your *uncle* Carter said that?" Savannah didn't know whether to be annoyed or grateful to discover that the man had been issuing orders behind her back.

"He's not really my uncle," the girl went on blithely. "He's Maddie's brother, but she said it's okay to call him that. She's going to marry my daddy, and then we'll be a real family."

Savannah had noticed the stunning diamond ring on Maddie's finger but hadn't realized Carter's sister was engaged to the ranch foreman.

"I'm going to be the flower girl and carry a basket of rose petals and wear a new dress and everything."

"That sounds like a very important job."

"Uh-huh. Pastor Jeb said it's the most important one."

Darcy's bright smile proved to be contagious.

"I wouldn't mind a little company if you're not busy right now," Savannah said. "It's been a little lonely around here this afternoon."

"Okay." Darcy was on the porch in an instant. She bounced into the chair and settled in. "Do you like animals?"

"As a matter of fact, I—"

"Good, 'cause there are *tons* of them around here. Goats and pigs and chickens—but you have to be careful because they'll peck your fingers if you try to pet them." Darcy examined the adhesive bandage wrapped around her finger, leaving no doubt in Savannah's mind that she was speaking from experience.

"I'll remember that."

"Daddy has been teaching me how to ride after school. Rambo is the sweetest horse *ever*."

Given the animal's name, Savannah would have to take her word for that.

"I'm going to get a pony for Christmas. It's white with brown spots so I'm going to call him Freckles." Darcy paused long enough to take a breath. "Everyone's going on a trail ride tomorrow morning and then we're going to have a picnic by the lake. Do you want to come with us?"

Savannah was touched by the invitation. "Not this time, I'm afraid. I'll have to wait until after my baby is born."

"When will that be?" Darcy stared at Savannah's belly with wide-eyed curiosity.

"February."

Darcy tapped the fingers on one hand, a look of concentration on her face as she silently added up the months. "That's not *too* far away."

To Savannah, it seemed aeons away…and much too close. Where would she be in three months? In three weeks? Not at the Colby Ranch, even though Savannah didn't have the heart to tell Darcy that. If everything went according to plan, she would be back in Dallas before Thanksgiving.

Spending another holiday alone.

The thought left a familiar ache in her chest.

Maybe staying here wasn't such a good idea. Although she hadn't met Carter's brothers, she'd liked Maddie and Violet immediately. What if being surrounded by Carter's family only made it more difficult to be alone again?

"Do you like kittens?"

"I've never had one." Savannah couldn't help but smile at the abrupt change in subject. Darcy reminded her of one of the songbirds she'd seen flitting from branch to branch outside the kitchen window while she'd brewed a cup of tea.

"Maddie and I found *five* of them living in a shed behind the barn. They get kind of lonely when I'm at school during the day. You can play with them if you want to."

"I just might do that." Savannah laughed.

Nanny to a litter of kittens. Well, she'd told Carter that she wanted to be useful!

"I've got a worksheet to do before supper. *Science.*" Darcy wrinkled her nose as she hopped down from the chair. "I better get home in case Uncle Carter comes back."

A masculine voice suddenly joined the conversation.

"Uncle Carter *is* back."

Chapter Ten

Carter caught Darcy as she jumped down from the chair and launched herself into his arms.

"What are you doing here, young lady?"

"I'm not disturbing Savannah, Uncle Carter," she announced solemnly. "She *asked* me to come over 'cause she was lonely."

"We can't have that, now can we?" Carter glanced at Savannah, who quickly averted her eyes.

And blushed.

He *knew* she would blush.

With her toffee-colored hair falling loose around her shoulders and a bright yellow afghan draped over her lap, Savannah looked relaxed. Content.

Beautiful.

Carter had heard her laughing as he walked up to the cottage. The sound had spiraled through him, a melody he had a feeling would stick in a man's mind for a long time.

He'd spent the day following Ricardo, Lupita's husband, around the ranch in order to give Savannah the space he'd told his family she needed.

Who was he kidding? The space *he* needed.

Because knowing a handful of details about Savannah's likes and dislikes…carrying around her photograph…wasn't nearly as dangerous to his peace of mind as having her right there. Close enough to breathe in the delicate floral scent of her perfume. Close enough to see the flecks of emerald-green in her eyes.

Close enough to touch.

"Uncle Carter!" Darcy tugged on his sleeve. "You're not listening."

"Sorry, squirt. One more time?"

Darcy released a patient sigh. "Savannah's going to take care of the kittens while I'm at school."

"That sounds like a lot of responsibility."

Savannah must have sensed he was struggling to keep a straight face because she leveled a stern look in his direction.

"You can show her how, Uncle Carter. You took care of them yesterday."

Apparently, he was going to have to explain to Darcy what the term *classified information* meant.

"That's different," he muttered. "Savannah is a civilian. I'm a marine. We're trained to—"

"Handle all kinds of situations?" Savannah finished.

"Right."

Darcy bobbed her head. "He knows how to put barrettes in. One fell out yesterday right before I got on the bus," she told Savannah.

"Very impressive."

Carter stifled a groan when he saw the twinkle in Savannah's eyes.

He could also fix an armored vehicle, but Carter decided that must not rank high in importance to an eight-year-old girl.

"And he—"

"Darcy?" Fortunately, Carter was spared from further embarrassment as Maddie's lilting voice drifted across the yard. "Where did you run off to, young lady? You've got some homework to finish before supper."

"Gotta go." With an engaging grin, Darcy scampered away. "I'll see you later, Savannah."

"Bye—"

The word hit the screen door as it slammed shut.

"It looks like you've already made a friend." Carter leaned against the door frame.

"So have you."

"Darcy's a sweet kid." Carter watched the little girl zigzag across the yard and dive into Maddie's waiting arms, proof of the close bond the two shared.

His sister had mentioned that Darcy hadn't always lived at the ranch. Ty Garland's ex-wife had died in a car accident and he'd become an instant father to a grief-stricken little girl he hadn't even known about before the tragedy. Ty had hired Maddie as a part-time nanny and Darcy had gradually come out of her shell, flourishing in the warmth of Maddie's love and attention.

Of the three of them, his sister's faith had always been the strongest, but she had always been focused on her career. So fiercely independent that Carter had never pictured her in the role of caregiver. But from what he'd seen so far, Maddie was a natural. Babysitting Darcy while Ty put in long hours at the ranch. Pitching in at the farm stand to help out Violet. Sitting by Belle Colby's bedside for hours.

Maddie was also quick to pull Carter into the family circle and ask his opinion on things, something she'd never done before.

You can't change the past. All you can do is move forward, with God's help.

Gray's words cycled through Carter's mind again, churning up the familiar restlessness that had plagued him since he'd arrived at the ranch. Carter seemed to be the only one having a difficult time leaving the past behind. And looking to God for strength.

"Darcy told me that Maddie's engaged to her dad."

Carter turned his attention back to Savannah. "Ty Garland. He hired Maddie to take care of her while he worked during the day. That's how they got to know each other."

Savannah tipped her head to one side. "But you don't approve?"

And here Carter thought he'd become adept at hiding his emotions.

"It's not that," he said slowly. "I hardly know the guy. He and Maddie have only been together a few months. The last I knew, she was supposed to marry Landon Derringer. You'll probably meet him within the next day or two. He travels back and forth between Grasslands and his office in Fort Worth."

"Meet him?" A frown creased Savannah's brow. "You just said that he and Maddie broke up."

"They did." He slid her a sideways glance to gauge her reaction. "Derringer's engaged to Violet now."

Maybe now she would understand why he'd done her a favor when he'd told everyone not to bother her. Savannah had enough on her mind without trying to figure out who was who. Especially with two sets of identical twins.

"*Another* brother." Savannah's wistful sigh stirred the air. "I'm trying really hard not to be envious."

"Future brother-in-law," Carter corrected. "And you're kidding me, right?"

"No." Savannah's eyes sparkled with sudden mischief. "And that, Sergeant Wallace, was *your* question for the day. Now it's my turn."

Carter stared at her in disbelief as she repeated his words from the night before. "The question of the day?"

"You said I could ask another one today, didn't you?"

Yes. Yes, he had.

"Fine." The word sounded grudging even to his own ears.

Savannah had a unique way of turning the tables on him. Making him see things from a different perspective. He just wasn't sure if he liked it or not.

"Don't look so grim," she chided. "I believe you just told Darcy that, and I quote, 'Marines can handle any situation.'"

True, but Carter was beginning to think it meant every situation that *didn't* involve a woman with sparkling green eyes and a smile that melted his defenses.

"What's the question?"

"When do I get to meet the rest of your family?"

Carter was beginning to regret starting this

"game." Savannah had a gift for asking the questions he preferred not to answer.

"Tonight."

"Really?"

"Maddie and Violet issued a formal invitation for you to join everyone for supper at the main house," Carter said reluctantly. "But are you sure you want—"

He stopped when Savannah's eyes lit up.

Well, that answered *his* question.

He'd been doing his best to avoid family gatherings for the past few days. The smile on Savannah's face told him that she couldn't wait.

"Are you sure I can't get you anything else, Miss Savannah?"

"I'm sure." Savannah smiled up at Lupita, who was hovering near her shoulder, a platter of homemade rolls balanced in one hand.

"All right." The gray-haired housekeeper looked a little disappointed as she moved to the next person seated at the table. "Elise?"

"No, thank you, Lupita." Elise Lopez had arrived just before dinner with her son Cory, who had peeked up at Savannah below the brim of a pint-size cowboy hat and offered a shy but adorable smile. "Everything was amazing, as usual, but I can't eat another bite."

"Good." With a satisfied smile, the housekeeper

swept toward the door. "I will be back with coffee and dessert."

"Just to warn you, Savannah—" Jack Colby lowered his voice to a stage whisper. "When you tell Lupita that you can't eat another bite, she doesn't think dessert counts."

Savannah could smile at the handsome rancher now that the initial shock had begun to fade.

Carter had said that his older brother, Gray, had an identical twin, too, but when the two men had walked into the dining room, side by side, it had taken all the good manners her grandmother had taught her not to stare.

Jack Colby and Gray were the same height and roughly the same build. Both had brown eyes and chestnut hair, although the styles were different. Jack's was on the shaggy side and a day's growth of stubble shaded his jaw, which Savannah thought only added to the man's rugged appeal. Gray was clean shaven, his hair clipped almost military short, like Carter's. Although Gray wore jeans and a flannel shirt, it was easy to tell which twin had grown up on the ranch because Jack's skin was stained a deep bronze from working outdoors.

Savannah's eyes strayed to Maddie and Violet again.

Two sets of identical twins.

It was a little surreal, seeing all four of them together at the table.

No wonder she got the feeling that Carter, with his wheat-blond hair and deep blue eyes, felt like the odd man out when he was in their company. The bond that had formed was evident in every smile that passed between them.

"I agree with Lupita. I don't think dessert should count, either." Keira Wolfe, Jack's fiancée, winked at Savannah across the table.

The slender blonde had been the last one to arrive, dashing into the dining room with a breathless "sorry I'm late—colicky horse" right before Jack had said a blessing over the food. After the prayer, she'd bounded over to Savannah's side and said hello, the welcome in her vivid hazel eyes as warm as the one Savannah had received from Carter's sisters the day before.

She'd been a little worried that supper at the main house would be a solemn affair, especially in light of what Carter had told her about Belle Colby's precarious condition and their mounting concern about Brian Wallace's whereabouts. Instead, conversation—and laughter—flowed as easily as the pitchers of mint tea that Lupita set at each corner of the mile-long table. Darcy and Cory Lopez sat next to each other, giggling as they tried to make words out of their pasta.

This, Savannah thought, was what a family was supposed to be like. Noisy and affectionate.

But she couldn't help but notice that Carter didn't join in. He didn't engage in the good-natured teasing or the laughter.

Savannah couldn't understand it. As an only child, she would have given anything to be part of a family like this. Before her parents divorced, she remembered silent dinners. And even though her grandmother's tiny home was filled with love, there had only been the two of them.

This was what Savannah had dreamed of.

What Rob had promised.

"Anytime you're ready to leave—" Carter's breath stirred her hair and Savannah suppressed a shiver as that unexpected jolt of electricity momentarily stopped her heart. It started thumping again, so loudly that Savannah was afraid everyone at the table would hear it.

"No." Her voice came out sounding a lot like the squeak in the screen door of the cottage.

"Okay, what are you two whispering about over there?" Maddie teased.

Savannah realized that everyone's attention was focused on them now.

"Is Carter telling stories about us?" Maddie's frown belied the sparkle in her eyes. "Because if he is, Gray and I know a few we could share about *him*."

"True." Gray leaned back in the chair and crossed his arms behind his head. "Like the time Mr. Holbrook hired Carter to cut his grass."

Maddie clapped a hand over her mouth. "I'd forgotten about that."

"What happened?" Violet's eyes glowed with anticipation.

"Here we go," Carter muttered.

"I think he was about eleven—"

"Twelve," Carter said under his breath.

Gray's eyebrow lifted. "Do you want to tell the story?"

"No."

"Then I will." Gray didn't seem the least bit intimidated by Carter's scowl. "Mr. Holbrook hired Carter to do his yard work and then went out of town for the day. Carter was supposed to use his push mower—"

"Mr. Holbrook never actually *said* what I was supposed to use," Carter interjected.

Gray ignored him. "All the kids hated to use it because it was one of those contraptions invented shortly after the wheel. And Mr. Holbrook had about two acres of lawn to cut." He smirked. "Anyway, when he got home that afternoon, he followed a line of tools up the driveway to the garage. Instead of using the push mower, Carter had souped up—"

"Fixed."

"—a riding lawn mower he had stored in his shed."

"One of the neighbors heard the commotion and almost dialed 911," Maddie added with a laugh.

She and Gray had everyone's attention now, even Darcy and Cory were listening.

"Why?" Keira asked. "Couldn't Carter put it back together?"

"Oh, my little brother got the thing running." Gray chuckled. "But he'd fixed the engine, not the brakes."

"In my defense, I did get around to it the next day."

It was the second time Savannah had seen that elusive dimple appear in Carter's cheek but the result was the same.

Instant tingles.

"*After* you took out his hedge," Gray pointed out.

"Did you get in trouble?" Cory's worried gaze swung back and forth between Carter and his brother.

"No way." Gray ruffled the boy's dark hair. "Carter was the neighborhood hero. Mr. Holbrook gave the push mower a one-way ticket to the salvage yard and everyone he hired to cut the grass after that got to use the riding mower instead."

"And people started to show up at our door, asking for Carter," Maddie said. "Dad couldn't even pull the car into the garage because it was filled with everything from lawn mowers to toasters."

"It became Carter's personal mission to fix anything that was broken."

Savannah fixed her eyes on her plate, unable to join in the laughter or meet Carter's eyes.

Was that what he saw when he looked at her?

Something that he'd promised to fix?

Chapter Eleven

"Is everybody awake?"

Darcy burst into the kitchen, almost colliding with Carter as he shuffled toward the coffeepot.

"They are now." Carter scooped the little girl up in his arms and gave her silky ponytail a playful tug. "You're up awfully early on a Saturday morning."

Darcy practically vibrated with excitement as he deposited her on one of the vinyl-covered stools at the end of the breakfast counter. "I couldn't keep my eyes shut anymore."

Funny. Carter had experienced the same problem—but for an entirely different reason. For once, it hadn't been nightmares that kept him awake most of the night.

He wasn't sure which was more dangerous to his peace of mind. The nightmares that continued to plague him…or thoughts of Savannah.

It hadn't escaped Carter's notice that she fit in with his family more than he did. After supper, she'd sat on the floor with a pillow propped behind her back and played a lively game of Chutes and Ladders with Cory and Darcy.

Watching her, Carter was convinced that Savannah was going to be a great mom. Her daughter would blossom the way that Darcy had under Maddie's loving care.

The difference was that Savannah's daughter wouldn't have a father like Ty to protect and cherish her. To slay invisible dragons underneath the bed and intimidate the teenage boys who would eventually ask her out…

The images that tumbled like dominoes through Carter's mind had brought him up short. The chances of Savannah giving him permission to be part of her baby's life were as slim as her letting him become part of *hers.*

Even if he wanted to be.

Carter had been relieved when his cell phone began to ring, providing the opportunity to escape for a few minutes. With everything that had been happening at the ranch the past few days, he hadn't returned his commanding officer's calls.

Sixty seconds later, he'd found himself wishing he hadn't taken that one, either. Carter had assumed the lieutenant would tempt him with another bonus if he agreed to reenlist. Instead, he'd been informed that his name had been officially submitted to receive a Silver Star.

Carter had said the right words and returned to the family room, wondering what he would say if Maddie asked him who had called. And why. The last thing he wanted was for Savannah to find out that he might receive a medal. A medal he might actually deserve if he'd saved her husband that day....

But Savannah had disappeared.

Maddie told him that she was tired and decided to call it a day. That she'd decided to leave before he could walk her home told Carter that she still wasn't completely comfortable in his presence.

Well, that made two of them....

"Are you going on the trail ride with us this morning?"

It took Carter a second to realize that Darcy was talking to him.

"I don't think so, squirt."

"But Lupita packed a lunch for us to take along and we're going to eat around a campfire like real cowboys." Darcy dug into the stack of pancakes Maddie slid on her plate. "It'll be fun."

"She's right, Carter." Violet sauntered into the kitchen, cowboy hat in hand, and made a beeline for the coffeepot. "It'll be good to get outside and clear our heads a little."

Carter was tempted to tell Violet that when he

wanted to "clear his head" he chose to go alone, not travel with a herd.

Maddie must have read his mind, because her smile slipped a notch. "Everyone is going, Carter."

"S'vannah can't," Darcy said around a mouthful of sausage. "I asked her but she hasta wait 'til her baby is born."

"I think I'll stick around here this morning." Carter sat down next to Darcy. "I've got a few phone calls to make."

A quick but knowing look passed between Maddie and Violet.

"What?"

"It's just that you can keep Savannah company if you're staying at the ranch," Maddie said casually.

They didn't think…

Carter swallowed a groan. Because the smile Violet aimed at Maddie told him they did.

"You're way off track. Savannah is—"

"Your friend?"

Rob's wife.

"Someone who needs a quiet place to stay." Emphasis on the word *quiet*. "Not a bunch of people getting into her business."

"She's lonely," Darcy said matter-of-factly. "Last night she said that we make her smile."

Insert knife and turn, Carter thought.

Violet brightened. "I've got an idea—" She pretended not to hear Carter snort. "She might not be able to ride, but the two of you can drive out to the lake and join us for lunch."

Carter didn't know what was worse. Maddie and Violet's matchmaking or their sneaky tactics to get him to be part of the family.

"Double trouble. That's what you two are."

Darcy giggled. Maddie and Violet looked as if he'd just paid them a compliment.

"Savannah might have other plans." Plans that didn't include him.

"She seemed to enjoy herself at dinner last night," Violet said.

Enjoy herself? Savannah's expression had reminded Carter of a kid looking through the window of a candy store.

Someone squeezed his shoulder. He glanced up, expecting to see Maddie, but it was Violet who stood behind him.

"I'm glad you two met and that you brought her here," she said softly. "I'm sure it brings Savannah comfort that she can talk to someone who knew her husband."

That's what Carter had thought—*hoped*—until the first time they'd met. Now he knew better. Memories of Rob weren't going to be a connecting point between him and Savannah. If anything, they were a wedge keeping them apart.

* * *

Savannah opened her eyes and blinked at the old-fashioned light fixture on the ceiling until it came into focus.

For the first time in months, she'd slept through the night. No doors slamming. No sirens or horns blaring. No trains rattling down the tracks.

Just the low murmur of cattle and the faint but unmistakable sound of…laughter.

Wrapping herself in the quilt, Savannah padded over to the window and peeked through the curtain to see what was going on.

A group of people had gathered outside the barn and she remembered that Darcy had said something the day before about a trail ride.

Savannah recognized Violet and Maddie immediately, working in tandem as they brushed one of the horses. Gray, who traded his khaki slacks for faded jeans and a long-sleeved T-shirt, stood next to Elise. Darcy and Cory were perched on the top rail of the round pen watching Jack bridle an enormous gray horse. Keira knelt beside the animal, running efficient hands down its length, lifting up the enormous hoof.

Savannah's curiosity piqued as a man led a coal-black horse from the barn. He paused and flicked the brim of his hat back.

Ty Garland.

It looked as if the entire family had set aside

their normal activities for the morning in order to spend time together.

Except Carter.

When Carter had left the room to take a phone call after dinner the night before, she'd seen Maddie glance at their older brother. The look of resignation and disappointment on Gray's face spoke volumes.

Savannah wasn't the only one who noticed that Carter held himself apart from the rest of the family. Gray and Maddie had told a humorous story from their childhood, but Savannah had read between the lines. Could see that the boy who'd kept his promises had grown up to be a soldier.

Carter was the kind of man people depended on. Looked up to. It was the reason he'd come to the ranch. He'd set his own feelings aside, his questions and confusion about the secrets his father had kept, because Maddie and Gray had asked him to.

And he'd invited her to stay at the ranch because she'd had nowhere else to go.

Carter's a good man, Lord. Help him see that his brothers and sisters are a gift from You. I pray that You'd bring his father home safely and that Belle recovers from her injuries. Bring healing to this family....

Darcy's squeal of delight brought Savannah's head up. She watched Ty swing his daughter onto the back of a buckskin horse that didn't so much as twitch with all the commotion going on around it.

Even from the distance that separated them, Savannah could see the camera in Lupita's hand as she herded everyone together for a picture. Violet planted a cowboy hat on Gray's head and Jack's shout of laughter scattered the chickens pecking the gravel. Ty's arm came around Maddie as they took their place by Darcy.

It was tempting to join them. Safer to hide behind the curtain.

This was a family it would be all too easy to fall in love with.

And not just the *family,* if Savannah were completely honest with herself.

She let the curtain swing shut and backed away from the window, afraid to let her thoughts continue down that road.

I'll take care of you, Savannah.

Rob had said the words and she believed him.

And even though she was beginning to realize that Carter was a man who could be trusted, she no longer trusted herself.

Carter watched Savannah brace one foot over the rail and lean across the fence to stroke Piper's nose. The mare whickered and nosed the pocket of her jacket, looking for a treat.

He took advantage of the fact she hadn't spotted him yet and took a moment to study her. The loose-fitting dress that was the exact shade of green as her eyes, her hair pulled back in a loose knot at the nape of her neck accentuating her delicate profile. And the pensive look on her face.

Guilt propelled him across the yard.

The group had set out half an hour ago, riding away in single file with Jack in the lead on an enormous gray horse.

Carter had checked his email. Twice. The house was quiet. Too quiet. He thought he would welcome the change, but the silence closed in around him instead. Along with the restless feeling that had become his constant companion since he'd returned to Texas.

"It looks like we're both temporarily sidelined, aren't we, girl?" he heard Savannah say. There was no resentment in her tone, only an undercurrent of laughter, bubbling below the surface like spring water.

"Her name is Piper."

Savannah's gaze lifted, and he saw a flash of disappointment in her eyes. "You didn't go on the trail ride?"

"I had a few things to take care of this morning."

"But what could be more—" Savannah stopped but the words dangled in the air between them, unspoken.

More important than family.

"You do have one question, remember?"

Carter tried to lighten the moment, but Savannah's eyes searched his face.

"That's not the one I want to ask," she said simply.

Carter felt a ripple of relief—and trepidation. It was his fault for bringing up that stupid game. The one *he'd* started.

Savannah seemed to have a gift for asking the one question that Carter didn't know how to answer.

Turning her attention back to the horse, Savannah combed her fingers through the tangled mane. Piper's liquid brown eyes drifted shut in absolute bliss. "I've never gone riding before."

Carter felt a stab of jealousy. For a horse.

No doubt about it, he was in trouble.

"Never?" He pushed the word out.

"City girl." Savannah shrugged. "My grandmother and I lived in an apartment that didn't even allow pets."

Carter filed that bit of information away. Rob had talked about Savannah, but never mentioned her family. Or his own, for that matter.

Why hadn't that occurred to him before?

"Does your grandmother still live in Dallas?"

Savannah shook her head. "She had a stroke two years ago and while she was in the hospital, she contracted pneumonia. The doctors couldn't get it under control with antibiotics and she…she passed away the next day."

"I'm sorry." Carter heard himself say the very words that had brought little comfort to him after Rob died.

"At least we had the opportunity to say goodbye. That made it easier."

Carter felt a strange tightening in his throat. The last time he'd been home on leave, over a year ago, his dad had asked him to hang out for an afternoon but he'd gotten a call just fifteen minutes after Carter had arrived. An emergency. Brian had been apologetic—told Carter that he'd make it up to him the next day—but Carter hadn't answered the phone. He'd grown tired of having his father's work schedule dictate their lives.

What if that had been the last time he'd spoken to his father? The email he'd written a few minutes ago remained in the in-box. Locked in the computer's memory like the emotions Carter didn't want to deal with.

"You must miss the city. It's pretty isolated out here." He steered the conversation to safer ground.

"No." Savannah shook her head. "I love the ranch. It's peaceful. There's room to breathe."

"I've heard Maddie say that, too. Five months ago, you wouldn't have thought she knew the front end of a horse from the back. The next thing I know, Gray will be bringing in cattle instead of criminals. He and Maddie both want to live here permanently."

Now why had he told her that?

Savannah tipped her head to look at him.

"Are *you* planning to stay?"

Chapter Twelve

One look at Carter's face and Savannah knew she should have chosen a different question.

"I'm sorry. It's none of my business." It really wasn't. But the more she got to know Carter Wallace, the more she *wanted* to know.

"You can ask me anything." Carter drove a hand through his hair. "I'm just not sure I'll always have an answer."

Which, Savannah decided, was an answer in itself.

Maddie and Gray were planning to make Grasslands their home and embracing the new members of their family while Carter prowled the perimeter, keeping a protective watch. Keeping his distance.

Well, there might be something she could do about that.

"When will they be back from the trail ride?"

"Not for a while. Maddie mentioned they'll be

stopping at the lake for a picnic lunch and campfire. Like real cowboys, according to Darcy."

"She was pretty excited about the trail ride today."

"Darcy gets excited about everything." The affection in Carter's tone affirmed what Savannah already knew. In spite of his feelings for the Colbys, the little girl had won him over.

"How far is the lake from here?"

His cobalt eyes swung back to her. "About a mile or so. You aren't thinking of walking out there, are you?"

"No." Savannah tamped down a sigh. "I doubt my doctor would consider a mile-long hike 'staying off my feet.'"

Savannah regretted the words when Carter's eyes narrowed.

"What do you mean? Are you supposed to be on bed rest or something?"

"Not...exactly."

"Define *exactly*."

"Dr. Yardley suggested that I cut back on my hours at the diner, that's all."

Savannah could almost see him silently connecting the dots.

"Is there something wrong with the baby?"

"The baby is fine."

Another heartbeat of silence followed.

"Are *you* all right?"

Something in Carter's voice suddenly made it difficult for Savannah to breathe.

"I'm fine," she managed to say. "My blood pressure was a little high at my last appointment, that's all."

"That's why you came here, isn't it?" Carter said slowly. "It wasn't just because of the apartment."

Savannah nodded reluctantly. "When I asked my boss if he would reduce my hours, he gave all of them to one of the other waitresses. If my next checkup goes well, I can ask him to put me back on the schedule."

"But won't the same thing happen again?"

"I'll be careful." Savannah rested one hand protectively against her abdomen.

"What caused this? Stress?" Carter obviously wasn't ready to let it go.

"Dr. Yardley said the same thing you did." Savannah summoned a smile. "That a change of scenery would be a good thing right now."

She wished she hadn't brought it up. She didn't want Carter to feel sorry for her.

What do you want him to feel? an inner voice teased.

Savannah elbowed it aside. Those kind of questions only borrowed trouble. Trouble she didn't need. In a week or so, she would be returning to Dallas and Carter would stay at the Colby Ranch with his family to wait for his father's return on Thanksgiving.

What was important now was to somehow help Carter see that he needed his family as much as they needed him.

"A change of scenery," Carter murmured, squinting at the horizon. "I could take you out to the lake to join up with the others. If you want me to."

Savannah struggled to hide her astonishment. And then looked down to hide her smile.

Thank You, Lord.

"I'd love to."

Savannah's initial confidence that she'd done the right thing began to erode with every bump and jolt that brought her into direct contact with Carter.

"Doing all right?" Carter glanced at her as the utility vehicle rolled slowly through the gully.

Define "all right," Savannah wanted to say. Because she was pretty sure that this time, the increase in her blood pressure didn't have anything to do with the fact that she was on her feet too long.

"That's where Jack lives." Carter pointed to an older, two-story home nestled between two mature pecan trees. "He moved in a few months ago and he's been fixing it up. Maddie said that he and Keira plan to live there after they're married."

Another couple who'd decided to make their home on the ranch.

"When will that be?"

"I'm not sure." Carter's expression clouded. "They're...waiting."

Savannah didn't have to ask, she knew what they were waiting for. For Brian Wallace to return. For Belle to wake up.

Carter slowed down as they passed the gate and Savannah saw the neat stack of lumber piled next to the stone foundation.

"It doesn't look like he's finished yet."

His jaw tightened. "From what I hear, Gray's been helping him on the weekends."

Savannah had guessed that he and his older brother had never been close, but that didn't mean it would be easy to accept Jack's presence in his life.

"Look." Carter aimed the vehicle at a wisp of smoke rising in the distance. "I think we found them."

The tiny man-made lake winked like a sapphire, a welcome oasis in the center of the windswept grazing land. Reins dangling, the horses stood, ground-tied shoulder to shoulder under a bouquet of cottonwood trees. A group of people circled a roaring campfire.

As they got closer, Savannah realized that everyone was looking at them, not the flames.

Violet rose to her feet and waved her cowboy hat as Carter stopped several yards away. "Look who's here! You're just in time for hot chocolate."

Savannah started to get down from the vehicle, but Carter was there before her foot touched the ground. His hand on the small of her back, guiding her forward over the uneven ground.

Savannah saw Maddie and Violet exchange a knowing look that she was afraid had nothing to do with some mysterious "twin" connection. It reminded her of the matchmaking gleam in Libby's eye the day Carter had walked into the diner.

Maybe this hadn't been such a good idea. She was glad when Gray immediately intercepted Carter and steered him toward the group of men standing around a portable grill.

"Sit down." Keira scooted down the blanket to make room for her. Elise already had the thermos open and was pouring another cup of hot chocolate.

"Yeah, now we can eat!" Cory pumped the air with one small fist as he and Darcy raced toward the adults.

Savannah glanced at Violet. "What were you waiting for?"

A smile played at the corner of her lips. "You and Carter."

"But...how did you know we'd be here?"

"Because we told Carter that he should bring you out here for lunch," Maddie said. "And no matter how he feels, my brother always does the right thing."

Savannah knew that, but for some reason, a knot formed in her throat. He hadn't run into her at the corral by accident.

This was what you wanted, wasn't it? For Carter to spend time with his family?

What difference did it make what had prompted his change of heart?

Because Savannah didn't want to admit she wanted Carter to seek out her company because he *enjoyed* it, not because his family had suggested it.

Not because he felt sorry for her.

"Did I say something wrong?" Maddie was looking at her closely now.

"No," Savannah said quickly. "It's just that Carter might have had other plans. I didn't come here to be a...burden."

To her astonishment, Violet nodded. "I know what you mean. When Landon showed up at the ranch and tried to help, I didn't want to accept it. I wanted to prove to him that I was capable. Confident. The kind of woman who could stand on her own two feet, like my mom. But you know what I learned? God puts people in our lives for a reason."

"Even when you think you don't want them there," Maddie added with a smile.

That's how Savannah had felt. At first. She hadn't wanted to admit that Carter been part of God's plan. And now she was afraid that he *wasn't.*

Maddie squeezed her hand. "I'm really glad you're here. You're good for my brother, Savannah."

Savannah froze, not sure she'd heard her correctly. "I don't know what you mean."

"Carter has always been a lone wolf. He separated himself from the rest of the family years ago. Dad was gone a lot and all of us dealt with that in different ways." Maddie sighed. "I think that's why Carter joined the marines right out of high school. I see how protective he is around you. It's obvious that he really cares."

"He—" *Cared about Rob.* "He's a good man."

"He's great with the kids, too," Violet said casually.

Too casually.

Savannah couldn't look at them now. It seemed that Violet and Maddie had a plan, too. To get her and Carter to spend time together.

"Is there anything I can do to help with lunch?" she asked.

Fortunately, Violet took the hint. She reached into the picnic basket. "Let's see what Lupita packed to go with the hamburgers Ty is grilling.

She had Ricardo drop the food off before we got here and then they were going to visit Mom at the Ranchland Manor for a few hours."

"How is she doing?" Savannah asked tentatively.

"No change," Violet whispered. "But we're waiting. And praying."

Savannah impulsively reached for her hand. "Sometimes that doesn't seem like enough...but it's everything."

Violet's eyes misted over but strangely enough, she smiled at Maddie.

"Would you like to go to church with us tomorrow morning, Savannah?" Maddie asked unexpectedly. "The service starts at ten."

"I'd like that."

"Great. There's so many of us, we carpool, so meet us in front of the house at eight-thirty."

Savannah's gaze drifted to Carter. He knelt on the ground next to Cory, eye to eye, listening intently to something the little boy was telling him.

He would be a good dad, she thought.

She wanted to ask if Carter would be going with them to church. But Savannah was afraid she already knew the answer to that question.

"Thanks for your help, Carter." Ty wiped the beads of sweat from his brow with the back of his hand. "It's always good to have an extra set of hands."

"No problem." Even though Carter had a hunch that his sister's fiancé could manage just fine on his own. Ty Garland had pulled him aside when they'd returned from the trail ride and asked if he would take a look at one of the four-wheelers that was being, in Ty's words, "a little cranky." All part of a plot designed to make him feel useful.

Not that Carter cared. Because it also kept his thoughts focused on a project and not on Savannah. Kind of.

When she'd admitted that the doctor had some health concerns, Carter had gone cold, struck by a fear that hadn't gripped him since the day he'd run toward the smoking convoy. During lunch, Carter had found himself watching her closely, looking for telltale signs of fatigue.

He couldn't imagine her going back to Dallas alone. Who would watch out for her?

God, please keep Savannah and the baby safe.

The prayer slipped out before Carter even recognized it for what it was. Something that used to come as easily as taking his next breath.

"Here's the wrench you needed." Ty waved it in front of his face.

"Thanks." Carter reached for it and saw Savannah walking back to the cottage from the main house. The women had decided to watch a movie together in the family room, an announcement that sent the men scattering like someone had dropped a stick of dynamite in the chicken coop.

Carter was the first one out the door, although he was glad Maddie and Violet had taken Savannah under their wing. He'd heard the three of them laughing about something right before Ty had pulled him aside.

Ty rocked back on his heels. "I know you're the mechanic, but I think it might work better if you use the wrench to tighten the bolt instead of *staring* it on."

Carter tore his gaze away from Savannah. "I was thinking," he muttered.

"Yeah." Ty's lips twitched. "I could see that."

Carter used the wrench with a little more force than was necessary. "You're good to go."

"I have to go into town and pick up a few things before the feed store closes," Ty was saying. "Want to ride along?"

Carter shot him a wry look. "How much is Maddie paying you to babysit?"

Ty grinned, not even pretending he didn't know what Carter was talking about. "I'm doing it for free, although she might have said something about apple pie."

"That's what I thought. I'll see you later."

"Maddie worries about you."

Carter had started to walk away but Ty's comment stopped him in his tracks.

"I'm a big boy." *A marine,* Carter wanted to add.

"You're also her baby brother."

"*Half* brother." Carter regretted the words as soon as they slipped past his lips. Regretted even more the look of disappointment that flashed across Ty's face.

"Does that change the way you feel about her?" he said evenly.

If they were going to talk about feelings, Carter was out of here.

"I don't know what Maddie's told you about our father, but he raised us to be independent." A quality that had made Brian Wallace's life easier. "The four of us haven't exactly been what you'd call close over the past few years."

"Maddie wants that to change." The look in the ranch foreman's eyes warned Carter to make sure he was willing to do his part to make that happen.

"I'm not used to having her and Gray fuss over me."

"I get that," Ty said. "It took me a while to realize how important family is. I almost lost Darcy because of it."

"I know Maddie wants us to be one big happy family, but it's a little difficult under the circumstances, don't you think?"

"If this isn't the time when you need family, I

don't know what is," Ty shot back as he hopped into the cab of his pickup. "I don't want you to make the same mistakes I did. When a man finds something precious, he holds on to it."

An image of Savannah's face rose in Carter's mind.

But she wasn't his to hold on to.

"Where does this go?" Carter hoisted the old metal toolbox up in the air.

"Why don't you put it the shed?"

Carter thought he heard Ty laugh as the window rolled up. Strange, considering how serious the guy had been a minute ago.

What did they want from him?

Grabbing the toolbox, Carter headed toward the storage shed behind the barn.

And almost tripped over the woman sitting cross-legged on the floor.

Chapter Thirteen

Savannah had been so lost in thought she hadn't heard the door open. But light suddenly spilled in and there was Carter, looming above her.

"What are you doing here?"

Savannah could have asked him the same thing. The last she knew, he and Ty had been walking toward the barn.

"Darcy is helping Lupita make cookies so I volunteered to check on the kittens." On cue, a tiny gray-and-white kitten darted from the shadows and attacked the laces on Carter's boot.

"Are you going to adopt one?" He scooped up the ball of fluff, his large hand forming a safe cradle. A moment later, the tiny body began to vibrate with a loud, rumbling purr.

"I can't." Savannah picked up the kitten's littermate as it rubbed against her ankle. "My next apartment might not allow pets."

The reminder that her stay was temporary cast a shadow over Savannah's heart. A sign she was getting too comfortable at the Colby Ranch.

"There's no rush," Carter said quietly.

Maddie and Violet had said the same thing when Savannah had asked if she could use the computer in Belle's office to check for new apartment listings in Dallas.

Savannah didn't have the heart to tell Carter's sisters that the reason they wanted her to stay was the very reason why she had to leave.

"I saw Ty leave a few minutes ago." As soon as Savannah said the words, she hoped the dim light in the shed would conceal her blush. Nothing like telling the man she'd been keeping tabs on him!

"He had to run a few errands after I fixed the four-wheeler."

"Maybe I should talk to Ty," Savannah said darkly. "Your sisters won't let me set foot in the kitchen unless I want something to eat—and then they insist I sit at the table while they make it." Even something as simple as microwave popcorn.

"Mmm." Carter bent down and set the kitten on the floor, his innocent expression instantly setting off an internal alarm.

"Did you have something to do with that?"

"I *might* have said your doctor recommended that you take it easy."

And he didn't look the least bit apologetic.

"I'm not made out of glass."

"You're a guest here, remember?" he murmured.

"How can I forget? You keep reminding me—and now everyone else."

Carter's laughter rolled over her. "Someone has to look out for you."

Savannah felt tears scald the back of her eyes and she buried her face in the kitten's downy fur before Carter could notice.

Rob had said the same thing. Savannah wanted to think she was a different person than she'd been seven months ago. That girl had been naive. Lonely. Susceptible to the charms of a man who'd used her vulnerability to his advantage.

Carter had never been anything other than straightforward with her from the first time they'd met. He'd told her the truth about what had prompted his invitation to stay at the ranch. She knew he was only following through on the promise he'd made to Rob.

She knew that every time Carter looked at her, he saw his best friend's widow.

The growing realization that she wanted him to see her as *more* than that left Savannah reeling. She leaned against the post before her knees gave way.

"It's okay to accept help, you know. You don't

have to go through this alone." Carter reached out and tucked a strand of hair behind her ear. His fingertips paused to linger on the sensitive spot below Savannah's jaw, where her pulse had begun to jump in time with the erratic rhythm of her heart.

His cobalt-blue eyes searched her face and a frown settled between his brows, almost as if he were seeing her—really seeing her—for the first time.

"Savannah—"

A low, mournful wail erupted behind them.

Savannah was already following the sound to the back of the shed. "I think one of the kittens got tangled in something."

Carter caught her hand as she reached for the canvas tarp thrown over an old piece of farm equipment.

"What did I just say?" He pulled the cover off and knelt down. Savannah hovered in the wings, watching as he disappeared beneath the tire.

"Are you pulling rank again?"

"Yes," came the muffled response. Carter extracted the kitten and deposited it next to its brothers and sisters, perched like a row of knickknacks on a low wooden shelf to watch the show.

"I don't believe it," Savannah huffed.

"Neither do I." Carter let out a low whistle. "Do you know what this is?"

Savannah followed his gaze to the vehicle that, like the kitten, had been trapped under the dusty tarp.

"A truck?"

"Not just a truck." Carter prowled around the front, his palm following every curve and line. "It's a '67 Chevy."

"Um, that sounds like a truck to me."

Carter's husky laugh sent the kittens scrambling for cover. If Savannah were smart, she would follow their lead.

"It *is* a truck. A classic." His enthusiasm was so contagious, Savannah couldn't help but smile as she ventured closer for a better look. "Who put you out to pasture?" Carter gave the truck's chrome fender an affectionate pat.

"Someone who wanted to *drive* a truck instead of push it?"

Savannah couldn't believe she was actually teasing him.

Carter flashed a boyish grin and patted the door. "Let's take a look at her."

"How do you know it's a *her?*"

"Too pretty not to be."

Carter threw open the doors to let in more light and the wind snaked inside the shed. Savannah shivered. Without a word, he stripped off his sheepskin-lined coat and dropped it over her shoulders. The heat from his body wrapped around her like an embrace. She caught her breath, trapping the tangy scent of his cologne in her lungs.

Carter slid into the driver's seat. He took a quick inventory of the interior, checking the glove box and running his hand along the underside of the seats.

Savannah spotted a set of keys hanging from a nail near the door. "Here. Try one of these."

The truck shuddered to life. And promptly died.

Which did nothing to dim Carter's enthusiasm.

"What's wrong with it?"

"I'm not sure yet," he murmured.

"Is that easy to fix?"

Carter grinned. "Easy, no. Possible, yes."

"I thought I heard someone in here." Jack's shadow blocked the afternoon sunlight streaming into the shed. "Hey, Savannah…and Carter."

"He was helping Ty. And I was visiting Darcy's kittens," Savannah explained quickly. She didn't want anyone to get the impression that she was looking for anything more than a place to stay for a few weeks.

"Uh-huh." Jack sauntered into the shed to take a closer look at what had caught their attention. "I forgot that thing was here."

Carter twisted around, a look of patent disbelief on his handsome face. "You *forgot?*" he echoed.

"It belonged to James Crawford. I remember he drove it in the Fourth of July parade every summer. It started to have issues so he must have put it out to pasture, so to speak."

"And you left it here."

Jack shrugged. "Ty and I have enough old junk to keep running around this place."

"Old junk?" Carter mouthed the words as if he couldn't bear to say them out loud.

"You're welcome to try—" Carter had the hood up before Jack completed the sentence. He winked at Savannah and dug a light bulb from a drawer in the storage cabinet. "The sun is going down. You might need this if you're out here all night."

Savannah noticed that Carter didn't contradict him.

"What's going on?" Maddie stood in the doorway. She'd changed out of her casual riding clothes into a long skirt, tall boots and a form-fitting suede jacket.

"Carter found a truck to play with," Jack quipped.

Maddie took a step forward, eyed the skeins of cobwebs hanging from the ceiling and stopped just inside the door.

"Violet and I are driving into town for a few hours to visit Belle. Pastor Jeb offered to meet us there so we can all pray for her. Do you want to come along?"

"Sure. 'Where two or more are gathered in my

name,'" Jack quoted softly, a verse familiar to Savannah. "I'll meet you out front in a few minutes."

"Great. I'm going to track down Gray and ask him, too." Maddie lingered in the doorway. "Do you want to come with us, Carter?"

Carter's head snapped up. "No, thanks."

An awkward silence descended. Jack looked as if he wanted to say more, but the set of Carter's jaw must have discouraged him.

It discouraged Savannah, too.

Because even though Carter had claimed she didn't have to go through difficult times alone, it was clear he wasn't willing to take his own advice.

The sun had set by the time Carter returned to the house. He'd heard the slam of a car door signifying his siblings return over an hour ago. By now, the family would be through eating supper and lined up on the sofa in the family room, watching football.

He shrugged off his jacket and padded down the hall. An inner voice taunted that it was pointless to check his email again but Carter ignored it.

They needed answers, and with Belle not showing any signs of regaining consciousness, there was only one person who could answer them. His father.

Now if only he could make it to the office before Darcy spotted him…

Carter's hand froze on the knob as he pushed the door open. Because he hadn't bypassed game time in the family room, he'd stumbled into some kind of family summit.

Which explained why he hadn't been invited.

Guilt reared up to pinch his conscience. Maybe because they'd asked him to accompany them to Ranchland Manor only a few hours ago and he'd turned them down flat?

Maddie and Violet sat in the window seat overlooking the courtyard while Gray and Jack paced the length of the room like a pair of caged mountain lions.

Conversation skidded to a halt when they spotted him.

"Sorry." Carter started to back up. "I didn't mean to intrude."

Gray cast an impatient glance his way. "You aren't intruding. We were waiting for you."

Carter's emotions shifted into high alert, the same way they had in Afghanistan when there'd been an imminent threat to the soldiers on base.

"What's going on?"

"Maybe you should shut the door," Jack suggested, his voice tight.

Carter closed the door and looked at Gray.

"Landon got here about an hour ago. I'd asked him to stop by the apartment and pick up my mail before he left Fort Worth."

For the first time, Carter noticed the envelope in Gray's hand.

"Dad?" Carter felt his lips form the word but he wasn't sure if he'd said it out loud.

"No." Gray hesitated, glanced at Jack. "A few months ago, Jack and I decided to have our DNA tested, to see if Patty Earl was telling the truth about Joe being our biological father."

Something else no one had bothered to mention until now.

"Was it necessary for both of you to be tested?"

"No, that was our decision," Gray said.

Another indication that the men had not only accepted each other, but were forming the same strong bond that Maddie and Violet had since they'd discovered each other.

"What did you find out?"

The brackets on either side of Jack's mouth deepened. "We haven't opened the results yet."

Carter didn't have to ask why. At no time since his arrival had Jack and Gray looked more alike than they did at this moment, when they had the answer to a pivotal piece of their past literally at their fingertips.

"You should open them when you're ready," Violet finally said.

Maddie rose to her feet and took both men by the hand. "A piece of paper doesn't change anything. It's not going to erase the memories we have of growing up together. Or the ones we've made over the past few months."

Gray stared down at the envelope with the same intensity Carter had seen on a bomb tech's face. Wondering what kind of shape he'd be in if he made the wrong call.

"There's nothing saying you have to open it now," Carter heard himself say. "Why don't you give it a few days?"

"Carter is right," Maddie said, stunning him once again.

Gray looked at Jack. "What do you think?"

"Yeah." Jack plowed his fingers through his hair. "I wasn't expecting the results to come back this soon. I wouldn't mind some more time to think about it."

"And pray about it," Maddie added.

"Why don't we do that right now?" Violet stood up and stretched out a hand to Gray.

Carter felt that familiar tightening in his chest as both sets of twins clasped hands and formed a tight circle. It wasn't just the similarities in their looks that made him feel like an outsider.

For a split second, Gray's eyes met his and Carter saw the question there.

Carter responded with a shake of his head.

And this time when he backed toward the door, no one stopped him.

Chapter Fourteen

"You're going to love Grasslands Community Church!" Maddie linked her arm through Savannah's as they walked to the car. "It's small and everyone knows everyone's name, so don't be surprised if they ask you a million questions. It's not because they're nosy—"

"Sure it is." Ty winked at Savannah as he opened the door of the backseat and waited for her to buckle up next to Darcy.

Savannah glanced out the rear window as Ty's pickup cruised down the driveway, but there was no sign of Carter. When Lupita fussed about him missing breakfast, Maddie and Gray had exchanged a solemn look but didn't comment.

Savannah didn't know if it was because he hadn't accompanied the family to the convalescent center or if something else had happened.

Right before she'd gone to bed, she'd heard a

door snap shut. When she'd peeked through the curtain, she'd seen a man sitting on the bench in the courtyard. Even in the dark, she'd recognized Carter's silhouette.

It had taken all Savannah's strength not to join him.

She'd prayed for him instead. Prayed that Carter would forgive his father for keeping secrets and let God heal whatever had caused the wounds in his soul.

The disappointment on Maddie's face when he'd refused to accompany the family to the convalescent center to visit Belle continued to weigh on Savannah's mind. While Gray and Maddie had made peace with the fact that Belle was their mother, to Carter she was a reminder that Brian Wallace had kept things from his family.

And Savannah knew firsthand just how painful secrets could be....

"That's the Colby farm stand." Maddie pointed to a one-story concrete building on Main Street. "I'm sure Violet would love to give you a tour. I've been helping out behind the counter once in a while."

"I wouldn't mind—"

"We're covered, Savannah." Maddie tossed a smile over her shoulder.

Savannah gave in. For now. But there had to be

some way she could feel useful without breaking Dr. Yardley's orders—or Carter's.

They passed a small town green, and Savannah spotted the church up ahead. With its white clapboard siding and slender steeple, it looked like a picture on the front of a postcard. Ty stopped by the doors to let them out.

As Savannah slid out of the backseat, she saw Violet hurrying toward them. The man at her side had no trouble keeping up with her, and Savannah saw a few heads turn in their direction.

She wasn't surprised. Violet and Landon Derringer made a striking couple. She'd met him briefly when he'd arrived the night before, just minutes before the rest of the family returned from visiting Belle Colby.

A reunion where, once again, Carter had been noticeably absent.

"Come on. We'll introduce you to Pastor Jeb." Violet tucked her arm through Savannah's as they reached the white paneled door.

People paused to greet her, and Savannah wondered what it would be like to live in a town like Grasslands. To have people know your name.

This was what she wanted for her child. A place to belong.

Violet waved at a tall, slender man standing just outside the doors leading into the sanctuary.

The minister was younger than Savannah expected, only in his late twenties or early thirties. A shock of russet hair matched the spray of freckles across his nose.

He smiled at Violet and navigated through the clusters of people until he reached their side.

"Pastor Jeb, this is Savannah Blackmore, my brother Carter's friend. She's staying at the ranch for a while."

Savannah hoped the pastor wouldn't read more into the "Carter's friend" description. She didn't want people to get the wrong impression about them.

Behind a pair of horn-rimmed glasses, the pastor's eyes were as welcoming as the church he served. "I'm glad you joined us for worship this morning, Savannah."

Two teen girls rushed over. "Did you bring something for the bake sale, Violet?"

"I brought one of Lupita's confections." Violet grinned. "How are things going in the kitchen? Do you need some help?"

"Yes!"

"I'll meet you in the sanctuary in a few minutes." Laughing, Violet allowed the girls to tow her down the hallway.

"Violet and Landon are really involved in Teen Scene, our youth ministry," Maddie said. "Landon's foundation funded a remodeling project last summer and the number of kids showing up on the weekends has doubled since then."

"That's a good thing, because we're going to need their help for the harvest dinner next weekend." Jeb plucked at his tie in a halfhearted attempt to straighten it that wasn't quite successful.

Savannah glanced at Maddie. "Harvest dinner?"

"Grasslands Community is putting it on, but the whole town is invited. It's a chance to come together and publicly thank God for the blessings He's given us. The whole family will be volunteering in some capacity…." Maddie's smile slipped a notch. "Well, most of us."

With a sinking feeling, Savannah guessed she was talking about Carter. "I'd like to help, too, if you're looking for volunteers."

"Always." Jeb smiled. "I'll introduce you to Sadie Johnson, the church secretary. She knows more about what goes on around here than I—"

A petite woman wearing a shapeless green cardigan and ankle-length khaki skirt suddenly materialized beside them.

"Oh, good, there you are! Sadie, this is Savannah Blackmore." Jeb wrestled his tie into place again. "She's staying at the Colby Ranch and would like to help with the harvest dinner."

A pair of bright green eyes blinked at Savannah behind oversize glasses. "It's nice to meet you," she murmured.

"Sadie's been handling most of the details so she can fill you in after the service," Jeb went on. "I don't know what I did without her."

Savannah was amazed to see twin swatches of color appear in the secretary's cheeks. Jeb Miller, however, seemed oblivious as he nodded at the usher who was waving a bulletin at them.

"I guess that's my cue." The pastor grinned, his tie flapping like a windsock as he loped away.

Savannah realized the prelude had started, beckoning the congregation inside the sanctuary. She followed Maddie down the center aisle to a pew near the front of the church where the rest of the family slid down to make room for them.

A feeling of peace swept over Savannah and she bowed her head.

God, thank You for bringing me here. Thank You for your presence. For the hospitality that Violet and Maddie have shown me…

The pew creaked as someone sat down beside her.

Savannah opened her eyes and slid a sideways glance at the latecomer. "Good morn—"

The whispered greeting died as she found herself staring into a pair of deep blue eyes.

The expression on Savannah's face told Carter that she hadn't expected to see him in church.

Well, he was a little shocked himself. He hadn't

planned to attend the service. The last time he'd attended church with his siblings was a Christmas Eve service shortly before he'd joined the marines. Their dad had promised to meet them there, but another emergency had come up and he'd missed it.

"Not everyone wants to be here this morning."

Carter's head jerked up as he heard someone voice his thoughts out loud.

The pastor, Jeb Miller, stood behind a wooden pulpit, Bible in hand.

"Some of you are worn out. Discouraged. Seeking. Maybe you've been running away from God. Maybe you're running to Him. But God brought you here—to this place—for a reason this morning. I trust that He'll reveal it to you."

Carter felt the words pierce his soul. He shifted in his seat, suddenly uncomfortable in a place he had once found comfort.

Savannah paged through the hymnal to the song listed in the bulletin. Her clear alto mingled with the other voices and Carter could tell she'd not only memorized the words, she believed them.

Maddie cleared her throat. The sparkle in her eyes told Carter she knew exactly where his thoughts had drifted.

He *knew* he should have stayed home.

When the song ended, Pastor Jeb tucked his

glasses in the front pocket of his shirt and opened up the worn Bible.

"Praise the Lord. Praise God our Savior..." His gaze lifted. Swept over the congregation. "Some of you might be wondering how that's even possible. Maybe you've been experiencing health problems. Maybe you've lost a loved one. Maybe you have to force yourself to get out of bed because even though the sun is shining, life seems...dark. You have doubts. Questions. Circumstances that make you wonder what there is to be thankful for.

"The rest of the verse gives us the answer." Jeb's smile encompassed the people around him. "*He saves us. He carries us.* No matter what we're going through, these are the things we can hold on to. God adopted us into His family—He saved us—and He'll never leave us alone...."

Carter felt beads of sweat pop out on his forehead.

Not here. Not now.

The flashbacks swept in without warning, like a flash flood. Something as ordinary as a word—or a sound—could release the images stored in his memory.

Carter's hands fisted at his sides. This was a part of *his* past he couldn't share with anyone. He swallowed the bile that rose in his throat, ready to bolt.

A hand covered his. Held him in place.

Anchored him.

His heartbeat began to even out and the haze lifted as Savannah's fingers twined with his.

Carter was dimly aware that the message was over and Pastor Jeb was closing in prayer.

He bowed his head, wondering how he'd drifted so far from his faith. Because it hadn't occurred to Carter that when he'd carried the wounded soldiers to safety, one by one, bullets striking the sand all around him, God had been carrying *him*.

Savannah rose to her feet, unable to look at Carter.

What had she been thinking?

He had never given any indication that he wanted her sympathy. Or her friendship.

But something Pastor Jeb said must have struck a nerve. She'd heard the subtle change in his breathing, saw his hands clench at his sides. Sensed he was about to leave.

She hadn't thought—she'd simply…acted. And now that the moment had passed, Savannah was going to have to face Carter again, afraid he would question why she'd taken his hand.

Afraid of what her answer would be.

"Got a second, Carter?" she heard Gray say.

Savannah quickly made her escape. Sadie Johnson was waiting for her in the hallway.

"Do you need to think about it for a few days, or

would you like to sign up to help with the harvest dinner now—"

"Now would be *great*."

Sadie gave her a curious look but nodded. "Okay. Follow me."

Savannah was relieved when the secretary bypassed the crowd of people milling in the hallway and turned down a narrow corridor to a small office tucked in the back of the church. Plants lined the windowsill and a large picture of Jesus, reaching for a lost lamb, hung on the wall.

"Is there a particular area where you'd like to serve?" Sadie handed her a clipboard and pen. "We need people on the setup crew and the hospitality team. I'm in charge of making the meal that night so I'll be doing a lot of the prep work that day."

"I worked at a diner, so I know my way around a kitchen. I'm not supposed to be on my feet for long periods of time, but if you give me a knife and a cutting board, I'm in."

Sadie paused to straighten a stack of papers on the desk. "This is Je—*Pastor Miller's*—way of filing things."

Savannah couldn't help but notice the secretary's tone sounded more affectionate than exasperated. She glanced at Sadie's left hand. No wedding or engagement ring.

"Do you have family in the area? Is that why you moved to Grasslands?"

Savannah had been making conversation, but Sadie shrank back as if she'd aimed a bright light in her eyes.

"Here's the sign-up sheet." She thrust a piece of paper at Savannah. "The youths are sponsoring a bake sale so I better make sure the kitchen is still in one piece."

"Sadie." Savannah took a deep breath. "I'm sorry—I didn't mean to be nosy when I asked about your family."

Sadie's shoulders hunched and her chin disappeared into the collar of her baggy sweater, reminding Savannah of a turtle pulling into its shell.

"It's okay," she murmured. "I don't like to talk about the past, is all. I'm in Grasslands because this is where God wants me to be."

Savannah felt an instant kinship with the woman. "I understand." She really did. "I'm here to help. With…anything."

For a moment, Sadie didn't respond. And then her lips curved in a shy smile.

"I can give you a quick tour of the kitchen now, if you have a few extra minutes," she offered.

Savannah smiled back. "I'd like that."

A few extra minutes were *exactly* what she needed. To get to know Sadie better.

And to avoid Carter.

Even though something told her it would take a lot more time than that to sort through the feelings he stirred inside her.

Chapter Fifteen

Ten steps away from freedom.

Carter maneuvered around the obstacles in his path—a gray-haired lady holding a plate of brownies, a young mother pushing a stroller roughly the size of an SUV, a teenager holding up a coffee can filled with donations—and kept his gaze trained on the target.

The front door of the church.

"Carter Wallace." Pastor Jeb's lanky frame suddenly blocked his escape route. "I hoped I'd get an opportunity to talk to you after the service. You've been on my prayer list the past few weeks."

"Thank you, Pastor." Carter dug deep and scraped up a smile. The red-haired preacher reminded Carter of one of the young chaplains he'd met overseas. Compassionate. Wise.

Dangerous.

The pastor's message had stripped away Carter's emotional armor, left him feeling vulnerable and exposed. And running for cover.

He took a quick surveillance of his surroundings, searching for the people he'd been trying to get away from five seconds ago. His family.

But now, when he could have used them as a buffer—or a shield—they were nowhere in sight.

"Everyone is checking out the bake sale in the youth wing." Pastor Jeb grinned, as if he'd read Carter's thoughts.

Dangerous, no doubt about it.

Carter weighed his options. Hang out with the preacher or join the people chatting in the fellowship hall.

"I'll wait here." Or outside. In the parking lot.

"Come with me." The pastor came up with another idea. "If you've got a few minutes, I'll show you what your sister's been up to."

"Knowing Maddie, it could be anything," Carter said as he fell into step with Jeb.

The pastor slid a sideways look at him. "I was talking about Violet. She and Landon have been working on Teen Scene, our youth program, for the last few months."

When was he going to start thinking of Violet as family?

It should have been easy, given the fact that she and Maddie were identical twins. There were similarities in their personalities, too. Jack Colby, on the other hand… The guy eyed him like he would a bronco trapped in a chute, as cautious about Carter as Carter was about him.

They turned down a narrow corridor that connected the sanctuary to another building.

"Landon funded the repairs so we could fix up this area for the teenagers after it was vandalized a few months ago. Every Friday and Saturday night, adult volunteers supervise the activities. Game nights. Pizza parties. You name it, we've had it." Jeb opened the door. "The kids congregate here after the Sunday morning services—"

The gym was empty.

"Well, they *usually* congregate here after the Sunday morning service," he said ruefully. "I guess it's a good sign they're all helping with the bake sale."

A door at the far end of the gym swung open and an adolescent boy with a shock of wheat-colored hair slipped inside.

"Tommy?" Jeb waved to get his attention. "Where is everyone?"

"The back parking lot. Jairo can't get his car started."

"Again?" Jeb chuckled. "I think he pushes that thing more than he drives it."

"I can take a look," Carter offered. "No one in my family seems to be in a big hurry to leave."

No one except him, anyway.

Tommy sidled closer. "You fix cars?"

"He can fix anything, kid." Gray had walked up behind them. "Cars. Armored trucks. Tanks."

Tommy's gaze swung back to Carter. *"Tanks?"*

"Sometimes."

"Sometimes." Gray cuffed Carter on the back of the head. "They give you a medal for modesty?" He lowered his voice to a conspiratorial whisper. "My kid brother can get a car without an engine to start."

"Cool!"

Carter rolled his eyes. "He's exaggerating."

"I hope you can fix it. Jairo is supposed to give me a ride home," Tommy added with a mischievous grin.

"You fix Jairo's car and you'll be a hero around these parts," Jeb said.

Carter flinched. There was that word again.

He followed Tommy to the parking lot, where a group of teenage boys circled a rusty pickup like mourners at a graveside service.

"This guy—Carter—he's going to take a look at the engine, Jairo," Tommy informed everyone breathlessly. "He fixes armored trucks. And tanks."

A lanky Hispanic boy stepped away from the vehicle, eyeing Carter with a mixture of skepticism and hope.

"I've got a few things to check on before I head over to Ranchland Manor," Jeb said. "Do you mind—"

"We're good." Carter was already bending down to take a look inside the engine. The boys crowded around him, blocking the light.

Ten minutes later, the engine coughed once and came back to life.

"That should do it." Carter wiped his greasy hands on a bandana one of the kids had tossed at him.

Savannah wouldn't want to hold his hand now....

Carter gritted his teeth in an attempt to channel his thoughts down a safer path.

A futile attempt, it seemed, because questions ricocheted inside his head.

Why *had* Savannah taken his hand? How had she known it was exactly what he'd needed?

"There you are."

Carter stiffened as a familiar face appeared in his line of vision. A familiar face whose brown eyes were shaded by the brim of a cowboy hat.

Jack.

"Maddie and Violet are going to help Sadie clean up from the bake sale and then we decided to stop over to Ranchland Manor."

To see Belle. Fortunately, Jack didn't ask if he wanted to go along.

"Okay. No problem."

"Can you give Savannah a ride back to the ranch?"

The two of them. Alone in the car on the drive back to the ranch.

Now *that* was a problem.

Savannah crumpled up the empty wrapper and licked a smudge of chocolate frosting from her finger as she left the fellowship hall to look for Maddie and Ty.

She'd stopped by the bake sale for a few minutes and ended up buying a piece of cake from one of the teenagers. Violet had been scurrying around the kitchen, helping Sadie, and Savannah had caught a glimpse of Keira striding down the hall, but at some point she'd lost track of the couple she'd ridden with.

She saw an open door halfway down the hall and slipped inside to look for a wastebasket.

Music drifted from tiny speakers mounted in the corners of the ceiling. Checkered curtains trimmed the windows. A padded rocking chair was stationed at the foot of a rainbow stenciled on one bright yellow wall.

The church nursery.

On their own volition, Savannah's feet carried her forward. She traced a finger along the rail of a wooden crib.

"It's amazing, isn't it? The smaller they are, the more stuff they seem to need."

Savannah turned at the sound of the pastor's voice behind her.

"I guess so." Savannah was three months away from her due date and hadn't set up a nursery yet. She had to find an apartment. Soon. Had to paint the walls and buy a crib. No matter what Maddie and Violet said, she couldn't take advantage of their hospitality much longer.

"We've got a wonderful group of volunteers to staff the nursery," Jeb said. "Your baby will be in good hands."

It was too dangerous to imagine being part of Jeb's congregation. Part of the community.

"I'm not staying in Grasslands very long."

"Oh? Violet made it sound like—" Jeb shook his head. "Never mind."

Savannah could only guess what Violet had made it sound like!

"I don't want to be a burden on the family."

"I know the Colbys pretty well," Jeb said easily. "I doubt they see it that way."

Did Carter?

That's what Savannah wasn't sure about.

Jeb turned off the CD player and for the first time, Savannah noticed the ring of keys dangling from his fingers. It suddenly occurred to her that while she'd been lingering in the nursery, the pastor was ready to leave.

"I'm sorry," Savannah stammered. "I didn't mean to keep you from locking up." Not to mention that Maddie and Ty were probably wondering what had happened to her.

"Don't apologize. I never want to miss out on a divine appointment." Jeb smiled. "God brings people together for a reason."

And hopefully, sometimes He kept them apart, Savannah thought as she made her way back to the foyer.

She pulled up short when she saw Carter prowling back and forth in front of the door as if he were waiting for someone.

The blue eyes drew a bead on her instead.

Heat swept into Savannah's cheeks even though she couldn't tell what he was thinking.

"Have you seen Maddie?"

"They decided to stop at Ranchland Manor and Jack asked if I'd take you back to the ranch. So I guess it's just you and me."

Savannah swallowed hard.

He'd been waiting for someone, all right.

Her.

Savannah kept her head down as Carter escorted her to the car.

It was clear he was going to have to have a

little talk with Maddie and Violet. Because this arrangement had their matchmaking fingerprints all over it.

Carter opened the passenger-side door for Savannah and went around to the other side. When he got in, she was trying to wrangle the seat belt into place.

"Need some help?" Carter automatically reached for the buckle and ended up holding Savannah's hand instead.

"Sorry—"

"—Sorry."

The words bumped together and the interior of the vehicle seemed to shrink in size, narrowing his focus to a pair of stunning green eyes.

As far as casual touches went, Carter had had more contact with a woman in the checkout line at the grocery store, but suddenly he found it difficult to breathe.

"Let's try that again." His voice was as uneven as his pulse. "The buckle," he added, just for clarification.

Savannah ducked her head as Carter snapped the metal clip into place but even though she wasn't looking at him, a new awareness shimmered between them, as warm and real as the sunlight streaming through the windshield.

"Thank you." Savannah's sigh fractured the

silence. "Some of the little things I've always done without a second thought are getting more complicated."

"I know what you mean." Carter spoke without thinking and then tried to cover the words with a laugh.

"Do they happen…often?" she asked softly.

Carter's gut clenched. No one in his family had questioned him about the flashbacks, although they probably wondered why he sometimes walked out of the room without a word of explanation.

"Often enough," he heard himself say.

"What—" Savannah hesitated "—helps you get through it?"

"If I can get away by myself for a while." Solitude didn't prevent a battering from the internal storm but at least when he was alone, his pride remained intact.

"Oh." Savannah's troubled gaze dropped to his hand and a hint of pink stole into her cheeks.

Carter suddenly had another flashback. Savannah taking his hand during the worship service, holding the darkness at bay.

That wasn't the way it was supposed to work.

He was supposed to be there for her, not the other way around. Keeping the promise he'd made to Rob, not fighting a growing attraction to the woman his friend had left behind.

Maybe a few hours spent tinkering with the engine of the Chevy would put things back in perspective.

He understood the way an engine worked. Knew exactly what to do when it didn't.

It was too bad life wasn't that simple.

He was about to put the car in gear when his cell began to ring. He glanced at the tiny screen and saw Maddie's name and number pop up. Anchoring the phone between his shoulder and his ear, he adjusted the rearview mirror.

"What's up?"

"Are you still at the church?" Maddie said breathlessly.

"Just leaving."

"I left my bag in the sanctuary. Can you check—"

"Sure." Carter swallowed a sigh.

"—and bring it to the convalescent home? We're there now with Belle."

Carter's hands gripped the wheel.

"Carter? Are you still there?"

"Yes."

"Thanks." Maddie seemed to think his response covered all the questions. "Belle is in room one-fourteen. We'll see you in a few minutes. Bye."

Carter heard a click in his ear. "Maddie left her purse."

"I'll get it." Savannah reached for the buckle on her seat belt.

"Don't take this the wrong way—but I can move faster than you."

"Is there a *right* way to take that?" Savannah muttered.

Carter grinned, feeling some of the tension between them ease.

When he entered the church, he saw a slight young woman about Savannah's age sitting in the front pew, her head bowed. He would have tried to sneak in, locate the missing purse and sneak back out, but the floor creaked beneath his foot.

Her entire body jerked at the sound and she twisted around. The church secretary. Sarah? No. Sadie, that was it.

"Sorry." *Whoa.* Carter backed up when he saw the tears rolling down her cheeks. "I didn't mean to startle you. My sister left her purse in here."

"It's on the table."

Carter looked to his left and recognized Maddie's purse. Of course it had to be *pink*. If the guys in his unit saw him now, he'd never hear the end of it.

He stuffed it under his arm, took a step toward the door and hesitated.

"Is something wrong? Do you want me to get Pastor Jeb?"

"No!" The word ricocheted around the room. "I mean, thank you—but that's not necessary. I'm…fine."

Yeah. There seemed to be a lot of that going around, Carter thought grimly. But he sensed that pushing the issue would only make the woman more uncomfortable.

He retraced his steps back to the car. Fortunately, Ranchland Manor was only a few blocks from the church.

"Maddie should be waiting by the door," Carter said as he pulled into the parking lot.

Except that she wasn't.

Five minutes ticked by and there was no sign of her or anyone else in the family.

Reluctantly, Carter parked the car and turned the key in the ignition, the engine dying along with the hope that Maddie was going to show up.

"I'll go inside and track her down."

To Carter's amazement, Savannah unbuckled her seat belt.

"I'm coming with you."

A nurse's assistant wearing bright yellow scrubs smiled at Savannah as she and Carter walked up to the desk.

"Can I help you?"

"We're waiting for my sister," Carter said.

"She might be in the family lounge. It's the second door on the left."

"Thank you." Carter was already on his way

down the hall, obviously in a hurry to complete his mission.

"There's no one here." Frustration leached into his voice.

"Do you know what room they're in?"

He gave a reluctant nod. "One-fourteen."

Savannah didn't have to work to keep up with Carter as they walked down the hall.

"This is it." Carter made no move to go inside.

The door was open a crack but Savannah couldn't hear the sound of voices. She knocked on the door and then gingerly pushed it open.

"They aren't here, either. Maybe they're getting a cup of coffee." Without waiting for permission, Savannah walked into the room.

A moment later, Carter followed. Fresh flowers bloomed in vases on the windowsill and someone had taken the time to fill the bulletin board on the wall with photographs of the family.

Savannah pressed her fingers over her lips when she saw Belle Colby for the first time.

Ribbons of copper hair spilled over the pillow, framing the woman's delicate porcelain features. Belle's eyes were closed, but Savannah just knew they would be the same shade of brown as Maddie's and Violet's.

Carter released a ragged breath. "Maddie… She looks just like her."

Savannah swallowed hard, trying to dislodge the lump that had formed in her throat.

What had Maddie thought the first time she'd seen her biological mother?

Belle moved restlessly and Savannah pulled the blanket up higher, tucking it around her shoulders. When she turned around, Carter was staring at the bulletin board. Someone had tacked a picture of Maddie and Gray alongside photographs of Violet and Jack.

"I don't understand why he did it," he said tightly.

Savannah knew Carter was talking about his father.

A soft moan from the woman in the bed brought both of them back to her side. Belle's forehead was furrowed and she tossed her head back and forth.

"Maybe I should get the nurse," Savannah whispered. "She seems agitated."

"Maddie said they talk to Belle like she can hear them," he said quietly.

Savannah's heart swelled as Carter reached out and took Belle's hand. An instinctive move meant to comfort the person who had turned his life upside down.

"It's going to be all right," he murmured.

The copper lashes fluttered in response to the husky timbre of Carter's voice. Belle's head rolled toward him. Her shallow breath took the shape of a word.

"Brian."

The color drained from Carter's face. "Did you hear that?" he said hoarsely.

"I...think so." Savannah pressed her fingers against her lips, certain her imagination had been playing tricks on her.

Carter stared up at her, his eyes dark with disbelief.

"She said my dad's name."

Chapter Sixteen

"Mom *spoke?*"

Violet was suddenly there beside them, Maddie, Gray and Jack one step behind her as they rushed into the room.

Carter shook his head. "I'm not sure she—"

"Did she open her eyes?"

"What did she say?"

The questions tumbled over each other. Carter didn't know which one—or who—to answer first. But the commotion caught the attention of one of the nurses in the hallway. She poked her head in, her expression a mixture of concern and disapproval.

"Is everything all right?"

"Mom said something." Tears glistened in Violet's eyes. "Carter and Savannah heard her."

"Can you describe what happened?" The nurse

moved toward the bed, her movements brisk and efficient as she began to take Belle's vitals.

Everyone was looking at Carter now, waiting.

"I'm not sure." Carter was already second-guessing what he'd heard.

Jack pinned Carter in place with a look. "What did she say?"

"It sounded like she said…Brian," he admitted.

Violet let out a startled cry and Maddie grabbed the back of the chair for support.

The nurse frowned. "Is that a name you recognize?"

"It's our dad," Violet whispered.

The room was silent as the nurse brought up Belle's chart and tapped something into the computer.

Jack finally voiced the question on everyone's mind. "Does this mean she's waking up?"

"I can't say that for certain," the nurse said cautiously. "But we'll keep a close eye on her today, and I'll bring it to the doctor's attention when he makes his rounds."

"I think I'll stay for a little while." Violet pulled a chair closer to the bed. "But the rest of you can go home if you'd like."

"I'm not going anywhere, either." Maddie brushed a strand of hair off Belle's cheek.

Gray pulled up a chair, and Jack propped a hip against the metal nightstand.

Apparently that meant they were staying, too.

Carter started for the door, prodded on by guilt.

"Are you leaving?" Maddie asked.

"It's pretty crowded in here already."

And he didn't belong. If—*when*—Belle Colby woke up, her family should be the ones at her bedside.

Carter forced himself to match his pace to Savannah's on the way to the parking lot. He opened the door for her and then slid in the driver's side. His fingers trembled as he stuck the key in the ignition.

"You didn't imagine it," Savannah said softly.

Carter's head whipped around. "Belle's own *children*—" he stumbled over the word "—have been talking to her for months. Praying for a sign that she'll come out of this and be all right. Why did it happen when *I* was there?"

"Maybe—" Savannah stopped.

He glanced at her sharply. "Maybe what?"

"You took her hand. Said her name. Maybe Belle heard your voice and thought *you* were Brian and she…responded."

"That's—" *Impossible,* Carter wanted to say. But then he remembered all the times that people had mistaken him for his father when he'd answered the telephone.

Could Savannah be right?

And had anyone else come to the same conclusion?

"She and Dad had been in their teens when they were together. They'd gone on with their lives. Why would Belle say his name?"

"Maybe there wasn't any closure," Savannah said after a moment. "She might…regret…the way things ended between them."

"Regrets." The word left a sour taste in Carter's mouth.

He had plenty of those. But did his dad have some, too? He'd married again. Had another child. Did he wish he'd stayed with Belle? Was that the reason he'd always seemed so distant? Buried himself in his work?

"You said no one knows why they split up. It could be that something forced them apart."

"Something like wondering whether Gray and Jack are really his sons?" The words slipped out before Carter could stop them.

Savannah stared at him. "What are you talking about?"

"Gray and Jack might not be my brothers."

"Of course they are. Look at Maddie and Violet."

"They resemble Belle—not my dad."

Savannah looked shaken. "That doesn't mean anything."

"Apparently Violet and Maddie met a woman in Fort Worth who claimed that her husband fathered the boys. Joe Earl and Belle went to high school together. So when it comes right down to it, they might not even be related to the girls by blood."

"I don't believe that. From everything Violet has said about her mother, Belle doesn't seem like the type of person who would have done something like that."

"It would explain why they split up," he ground out.

"Wouldn't a DNA test rule that out?"

"Gray and Jack took one while I was overseas. The results are back but they aren't ready to look at them yet. I guess they're not ready to deal with the ramifications of it."

"Or they already have," she murmured.

Carter parked the car in front of Savannah's cottage and turned to look at her. "What do you mean?"

"Maybe they decided it doesn't matter."

Savannah stared out the window.

The main house remained dark. Lights blazed from the window of the shed where Carter had discovered the truck.

It had been several hours since he'd dropped her off at the front door and she'd spent a lot of time in prayer.

There were things she might never understand about the past, but she was determined to trust God's plan, for her and her unborn child. She thought she'd lost everything when her husband walked out, but the baby had been a gift from God. An unexpected blessing that had encouraged her to keep going. To keep trusting.

She prayed Carter would begin to trust Him, too. Understand how blessed he was to have a family who loved him.

But right now, he was alone.

Savannah grabbed her jacket and went outside.

The door was closed to hold the chill at bay but a country ballad rattled the walls, trying to escape.

Now that she was here, she was having second thoughts.

Carter hadn't sought out her company, which meant that he preferred to be alone.

Or it had become a habit.

The door opened and Carter stood there, effectively shutting off all thoughts of retreat.

"Come on in. It's cold outside."

"How did you know I was here?"

He raised an eyebrow.

"Marine. Right."

To Savannah's absolute amazement, Carter's elusive dimple surfaced, giving her the courage to venture inside.

"Did you get the truck running yet?"

"Are you familiar with the old saying 'good things come to those who wait'?"

"Uh-huh. So that means it's still broken."

"Not broken." Carter reached into the engine. "A work in progress."

Savannah reached out to pet one of the kittens, who'd commandeered the jacket Carter had tossed on a chair.

"Did you eat supper at the main house?" Carter asked.

"No one's back yet."

Carter went still. "They're still at the convalescent home?"

"I think so."

Carter didn't say anything, but Savannah could see that he blamed himself for that.

"They're where they want to be, Carter."

And if she were completely honest, so was she.

"Can I help?"

Carter looked as surprised by Savannah's impulsive offer as she was to have made it.

"What do you know about trucks?"

"I know when you put the key in the ignition and step on the gas they're supposed to go."

"Then no, you can't help. But you *can* follow your doctor's orders." Carter yanked a chair into the light and swiped at the upholstered seat, an invitation to stay that Savannah didn't hesitate to accept.

For the next half hour, she watched him work, humming along with the radio or muttering under his breath, depending on what was going on underneath the hood.

A slow country song, as much a classic as the truck Carter was trying so hard to resuscitate, drifted from the speakers of the dusty radio parked in a corner of the shed.

The toe of Savannah's shoe tapped the dusty floor, and it caught Carter's attention.

"You're a fan?"

"Uh-huh, but I'm not sure how it happened. At the diner, Bruce either had a country music station blaring from the radio, or a football game. I tried to fight it—"

"And ended up liking both." Carter grinned.

"Exactly." Savannah couldn't resist grinning back.

"In that case—" Carter held out his hand "—would you care to dance, ma'am?"

"I can't...dance."

Savannah backed away from Carter as if he'd offered her a stick of dynamite.

"Everyone can dance." For his own sake, Carter hoped he was right.

"My balance is off. I can hardly walk a straight line anymore."

"Swaying...dancing...they're kind of the same thing, aren't they?" Carter had been teasing—until he saw the wary look return. Carter still didn't know what Rob had done to put that expression there but he wanted to do something to extinguish it. For good.

He drew Savannah into his arms and ignored her chirp of protest, surprised at how good—how right—it felt to have her there.

The top of her head grazed Carter's chin and the delicate floral scent of her shampoo reminded him of spring.

"See?" he murmured close to her ear.

She promptly stepped on his foot.

"I warned you that would happen."

Carter smiled. "What happened?"

"You'll know when the bruise shows up," she muttered. "I'm not exactly graceful anymore."

"You're beautiful." The words slipped out before Carter could stop them.

Savannah averted her gaze. "You don't have to do this, you know."

"Do what?"

"Tell me what you think I want to hear."

Is that what Rob had done? Just because they'd been good friends didn't mean that Carter was unaware of Rob's weaknesses. The guy could have sold fertilizer to a rancher.

Suddenly, Carter wanted her to see *him,* not Rob.

"I'm telling you the truth." He cupped the delicate curve of her jaw and lifted her face. Pressed a kiss against her forehead.

Savannah stared up at him, her eyes wide with shock. And something else; something that made his heart trip.

Carter's hands settled on Savannah's waist and he dipped his head, capturing her lips in a lingering kiss that she sweetly returned.

Something moved under his palm and Carter jerked back in surprise. *"What—"*

Color flooded Savannah's cheeks. "The baby is pretty active this time of the day. Sometimes I'm convinced that she's going to be a professional soccer player."

If Carter had ever questioned how Maddie and Gray could feel so…*connected*…to Belle, a woman they'd never met, he understood it now, when he felt another tiny flutter, as delicate as the brush of a butterfly's wing, against his palm.

Carter wanted to take care of *both* of them, and not because of the promise he'd made to a friend. Somewhere along the way, Savannah and the baby had become linked together in Carter's mind. And in his heart.

"Savannah—"

"Uh-oh." A teasing sparkle lit Savannah's eyes. "Why do I get the feeling that you're about to ask your question of the day?"

"What happened between you and Rob?"

Carter felt the tremor that ran through Savannah and she slipped out of his arms. He felt the chill of her retreat the moment she stepped away.

For a moment, he didn't think she was going to respond. And Carter was already regretting that he'd shattered the closeness of the moment by bringing up the past.

"I—I worked the closing shift at the diner and Rob came in one night. The other waitresses actually argued over who would get to wait on him because he was so good-looking.

"I was bussing tables that night, so I stayed out of it. Rob knocked a glass of water over and insisted that I let him help me clean it up. He told me later that he'd done it on purpose in order to meet me."

So far, that sounded like Rob, Carter thought wryly.

"He told me that he was in medical school and needed a quiet place to study."

That didn't. "Medical school?"

"To become a pediatric surgeon."

Carter frowned. "Rob never mentioned that he wanted to be a doctor."

"Because he didn't. He made it up to…impress me. Rob never even finished high school. When we met, he was working for a cleaning service. He stopped at the diner before his shift started and ordered a cup of coffee because it was all he could afford, not so he could stay awake all night studying."

"Why didn't he just tell you the truth?"

"Believe it or not, I asked Rob the same question. He didn't think I would be interested in a high school dropout so he made up all these stories to win me over." Her voice quivered with emotion. "I didn't ask for details, I just—"

"Trusted him."

Savannah nodded. "My grandmother was gone and I didn't have any family. It was easy to ignore the red flags and let Rob sweep me off my feet. He said if we loved each other, there was no reason to wait to get married." She swallowed hard. "Looking back, I think he was afraid I would find out the truth and leave—but he left *me,* a week after we got married. We had a huge argument. He said that marrying me had been a…mistake."

None of this lined up with the guy Carter had known.

"Is that why you didn't tell Rob about the baby?"

Savannah flinched. "I didn't know I was pregnant right away. I thought the symptoms, what I was feeling, was caused by…stress. When I finally went to the doctor, I was already four months along. I sent Rob an email, asking him to c-call me, but it was too late."

Carter did the math and released a ragged breath. Would it have made a difference, if his friend had known about the baby? Would Rob have taken steps to reconcile with Savannah?

"I wanted to work things out," Savannah went on in a low voice. "I was hoping that when Rob found out I was pregnant, it might make a difference. That he would give our marriage another chance."

Carter felt as if he'd just been sucker punched. "You would have taken him back?"

"I may have rushed into getting married, but I took the vows seriously." Savannah searched his face. "You still don't believe me, do you?"

She pivoted away from him and walked out the door.

Carter let her go.

Because he was the one who should have died when the convoy was attacked.

Rob hadn't been given another chance.

But for some reason, *he* had.

If only Carter knew what he was supposed to do with it.

Chapter Seventeen

"Mail call." Violet breezed into the kitchen where Savannah sat at the breakfast counter, frosting a cake for the harvest dinner. With a little coaxing, Lupita had agreed to let her help out and this was the only job the housekeeper decided wouldn't be too taxing.

"The house is pretty quiet today. Where is everyone?" Violet hopped onto the stool next to Savannah and eyed the bowl of cream cheese frosting. "That looks yummy."

"Carrot cake. Lupita made three of them for tonight."

"I suppose Maddie isn't home from work yet, is she?"

"Not yet."

"This one goes to the bottom of the pile then." Violet sifted through the stack of envelopes. "Carter?"

The knife Savannah had been holding almost slipped out of her hand. "N-no."

"He must be helping Ty again today. I know he wants to feel useful, but I'm beginning to think we're taking advantage of him." She furrowed her brow. "I haven't seen much of him the past few days so he must have found something to keep himself busy."

Or else, Savannah thought, Carter was avoiding her. It was a little hard to tell, given the fact that she'd been avoiding *him.*

But keeping her distance hadn't stopped Savannah from thinking about the kiss they'd shared.

She ducked her head, hoping Violet wouldn't notice the color stealing into her cheeks.

Violet surreptitiously swiped her finger around the rim of the bowl. "Sadie stopped by the produce stand this morning and said you're planning to meet her at the church."

"She has some last-minute prep work for the harvest dinner." And Carter wasn't the only one who wanted to feel useful. "Making the stuffing. Getting the turkeys in the oven—"

"Peeling the hundred pounds of potatoes I donated." Violet grinned. "Keira and I signed on to set up the tables, so we'll swing by later this afternoon. Gray picked up Elise and Cory and they're on the way to Grasslands as we speak."

"What about Landon?" Savannah teased.

"He had a project to finish up, but he'll be here, too."

Savannah wasn't surprised to hear that everyone had adjusted their schedules so they could help with the dinner. Both the community and the congregation had rallied around the family over the past few months and the event provided a way for them to give back.

"Something smells good." Jack wandered into the kitchen, looking every inch the cowboy in a canvas work coat, faded jeans and leather boots.

"Carrot cake." Violet pushed the bowl of frosting toward him.

Jack reached for it, spotted the mail on the counter and flicked a questioning look at his sister.

"Nothing," Violet said gently. "Darcy got a card from her grandparents and there's a letter for Carter. Looks kind of official."

Jack nodded. "Gray mentioned something about him being nominated for a medal."

"A medal?"

Two pairs of brown eyes cut to Savannah and she realized she'd said it out loud.

"The Silver Star. Apparently Carter saved three men during an ambush a few months ago, one of them a high-ranking officer who was visiting the base. He risked his life to get them to safety."

"I can't believe he didn't tell us that," Violet murmured. "That's quite an honor."

"An honor Carter doesn't think he deserves, according to Gray."

"Why—"

Savannah saw Jack shake his head and Violet lapsed into silence.

That's when she knew.

The ambush they were talking about…it had to be the one that claimed Rob's life.

"Excuse me." Savannah slid off the stool and felt her knees wobble. "Sadie's waiting. I should probably go."

Violet caught her hand and squeezed it.

"I'm sorry, Savannah. I wasn't thinking." Violet bit her lip. "I didn't mean to remind you of something so painful."

"I know. And you *should* be proud of Carter. He's a hero."

He always does the right thing, Maddie had said.

Risking his life for a fellow soldier.

Or keeping a promise to the one he hadn't been able to save.

Sadie was already stationed at the sink when Savannah arrived at the church.

"You should have told me you'd be here early."

"I had some extra time so I thought I might as

well get to work." Sadie nodded in the direction of an enormous plastic bucket.

Violet's potatoes.

Savannah grabbed an apron from the hook near the door and tied it around what remained of her waist.

The side door of the kitchen swung open and a teenage boy with shaggy black hair prowled in.

"What do you need, Jairo?" Sadie asked calmly.

"Is there anything to drink?"

"Lemonade in the fridge." Sadie gave him an indulgent smile. "And if you promise not to track in any more dirt, I'll throw in some of these cookies."

"Deal." Jairo flashed a boyish grin at odds with his tough exterior and tiptoed across the kitchen floor.

"How is it going out there?" Sadie began to pile cookies on a plate.

"We're working on the brakes right now. Carter has to order a part, but he thinks it will be here by the end of the week."

The potato Savannah had been peeling slipped out of her hand and landed in the sink with a thud. "Carter *Wallace?*"

"*Sí.* He's helping us." Jairo snagged a cookie from the plate, dodging Sadie's playful slap to the back of his hand. "Gotta go. They're waiting for me."

After Jairo left the kitchen with the refreshments, Savannah tried to wrap her mind around the fact that Carter was here. At the church.

Sadie didn't seem to notice how flustered she was.

"Jeb..." The receptionist caught herself. "*Pastor* Jeb said that Carter Wallace donated an old truck to Teen Scene so the boys will have something to keep them busy after school."

"An old truck?"

"It's an antique, I guess. I can't remember what he said it was."

"A '67 Chevy."

Sadie's eyes widened. "That's right. Have you seen it?"

Savannah had not only seen it, she'd seen the look on Carter's face when he'd discovered it in the shed. And yet he'd donated it to the church. Volunteered to help the boys fix it up.

"You don't mind running a plate of sandwiches out there, do you? I've seen the way those boys eat and they're going to need more than a handful of cookies to tide them over until the dinner tonight." Sadie handed her a platter.

"I—" Savannah tried to come up with a reasonable excuse to decline.

"Go on." Sadie gave her a gentle nudge. "The setup crew will be here in a few minutes so I have to be here to tell them what to do."

Savannah somehow found herself on the other side of the door.

Her steps slowed as she spotted Carter, surrounded by a pack of boys who appeared to be listening intently to his instructions.

In a camouflage jacket and loose-fitting jeans the faded blue of an April sky, Carter looked confident and in control.

And way too appealing.

Carter handed Jairo a tool and the boy beamed as if he'd been given a medal.

A Silver Star...doesn't think he deserves it.

Jack's words cycled through Savannah's mind again and she suddenly realized why.

Carter blamed himself for Rob's death.

Savannah stumbled, wondering why it hadn't occurred to her before. But she knew without a doubt that Carter would have done everything possible to save Rob. The fact he'd put his own life at risk to save the other soldiers showed the kind of man he was.

The kind of man it would be all too easy to fall in love with.

"Food!"

Carter had just shimmied under the truck when he heard a muffled cheer and the clatter of tools hitting the ground around him.

It appeared he was going to have to lecture the

kids on their priorities. Because they'd just abandoned an icon for an afternoon snack.

Sadie must have taken pity on them.

Out of the corner of his eye, he saw a dozen pairs of size eleven tennis shoes…and one pair of dainty blue ones.

Savannah.

Carter jerked. His forehead connected with the undercarriage and he growled.

"Are you all right?" Savannah was on her knees, peering under the vehicle.

"I'm fine." At least he would be. Once the spots in front of his eyes went away.

"I don't believe you. Your face is all scrunched up like you're in pain."

"Marines don't feel pain." He pulled in a breath. "And we don't…*scrunch.*"

"You're bleeding."

That got the attention of the boys, who momentarily abandoned their snack and hustled over for a better look.

"Cool!" Tommy breathed.

Carter felt a trickle of *something* run down his cheek.

"I'll get the first-aid kit." Savannah was already pushing to her feet.

"Don't you dare." Carter rolled out from under the vehicle and pressed the hem of his shirt to his temple.

"You might have a concussion."

"I don't have a—" Carter's breath snagged in his throat as Savannah stood on her tiptoes to examine the tiny scratch on his forehead.

"It's not deep," she murmured.

Carter was close enough to see the lavender shadows beneath her eyes.

Close enough to kiss her again.

His gaze dropped to the full curve of her bow-shaped lips and he swayed a little.

Maybe he *did* have a concussion. Or maybe his subconscious was reminding him how right she'd felt in his arms.

Savannah's hands reached out to steady him and the contact sent another jolt of awareness rocketing through his veins.

He took a step backward to put some distance between them.

"You look tired," he said bluntly. "I think you should be on the sofa with your feet up, reading a book."

"Really?" Savannah crossed her arms. "And I think you should be at the clinic. This cut might need stitches."

The boys, who had drifted away, perked up their ears at that.

"I don't need—" Wait a second. "You're doing this on purpose."

"Doing what on purpose?"

"*Fussing* over me."

"Fussing?" Savannah blinked, as innocent as one of Darcy's kittens.

"Giving me a taste of my own medicine, so to speak." Carter's eyes narrowed. "You are under no obligation to worry about me. But I—" He stopped.

"Have an *obligation* to worry about me."

Carter tried not to let Savannah see how the words affected him.

How *she* affected him.

Over the past two weeks, the promise he'd made to Rob had undergone a subtle change. Now, instead of looking out for her, Carter looked forward to spending time *with* her.

Which was why he'd tried to put some distance between them the past few days. A plan that had backfired. Just because he hadn't seen much of Savannah didn't mean he'd stopped thinking about her.

Or the way she'd returned his kiss.

The one he'd had no business initiating. The one he had no business repeating.

"I told you before that I'm not your responsibility," Savannah said slowly. "But here's my promise to you—I'll be leaving soon, and you won't have to worry about me anymore."

Carter didn't miss the irony. The government

wanted to give him an award for bravery but he was afraid to tell Savannah the truth.

He wanted her to stay.

Chapter Eighteen

The church kitchen was bustling with activity by the time Savannah returned.

Praise music played in the background, a sweet accompaniment to the chatter of conversation as everyone set to work. Maddie and Violet were working in tandem, chopping up fresh vegetables for the teenage girls who were making up the trays.

The phone began to ring and Elise reached for it. "Grasslands Community Church." She put her hand over the mouthpiece. "Does anyone know where Sadie went?"

Kiera glanced up. "I saw her a few minutes ago. She said she was going to look through the storage closet and round up the centerpieces for the tables."

"Sally has a question about the pies."

"I'll find her," Savannah offered. It would give her a few minutes to collect herself.

The unexpected encounter with Carter had left her shaken.

Savannah didn't like secrets—but realizing she'd fallen in love with a man who only saw her as his best friend's widow wasn't one she could share with the women gathered together in the kitchen.

Savannah heard voices down the hall as she rounded the corner.

Pastor Jeb and Sadie. They stood at the end of the hall and Savannah started in that direction. She saw Jeb touch Sadie's arm. With an anguished cry, Sadie jerked away from him and fled down the hall.

Right toward Savannah.

"Sadie! Wait!"

But the other woman streaked past her, tears streaming down her cheeks.

Jeb started after her but Savannah blocked his path. "What's going on?" In spite of what she'd just witnessed, Savannah couldn't believe that Jeb was capable of a harsh word.

"I didn't mean to upset her." Jeb winced when they heard a door slam. He looked discouraged. Defeated.

Two emotions that Savannah wouldn't have expected him to display, either.

"Was it bad news?" she asked cautiously. She didn't want to pry, but she was concerned about her new friend.

Jeb's lips twisted. "I guess so," he muttered.

Savannah didn't understand the cryptic comment. "I'll find Sadie and make sure she's all right."

Jeb scrubbed a hand across his jaw. "I guess that would be best, under the circumstances."

What circumstances? Savannah wanted to know. But she gave the pastor's arm a reassuring pat. "Can you let Maddie and Violet know I'll be back in a few minutes?"

"Sure." Jeb's gaze strayed to the door again. "Thanks, Savannah."

She had a hunch she knew where Sadie would go. Sure enough, she stepped out the back door of the church and spotted her sitting on a bench under one of the trees in the prayer garden.

"Sadie?"

Sadie's head jerked up and she rose to her feet, poised to flee again. The panic in her eyes subsided a little when she saw Savannah approaching.

"I'm sorry I ignored you." Sadie's voice wobbled. "I just needed…some air."

"No apology's necessary." Savannah drew her back down to the bench. "What did Pastor Jeb say to upset you?"

A sniffle followed the question. Sadie twisted

her fingers together in her lap. "The dinner…Pastor Jeb asked me to go."

Savannah frowned. "The harvest dinner?"

Sadie bobbed her head.

"Of course you'll be there. Why would he ask you that?"

"He—" Another sniffle. "Asked me to go *with* him."

"Like a…date?"

"Yes!" Sadie wailed.

It was all Savannah could do to wrestle back a smile, but the anguished look on Sadie's face told her that this wasn't the time to tease.

"He likes you," she said cautiously. "Isn't that a good thing?"

"It's *terrible.*" Sadie's shoulders wilted. "I didn't lead Jeb on. I have no idea why he would be—"

"Attracted to you?" Savannah pulled a clean tissue from her apron pocket and handed it to the other woman.

"Yes. I mean, just…*look* at me."

"I am." Savannah smiled now. "You care about people. You're pretty and smart and sweet and kind—"

"I'm none of those things." Sadie's voice barely broke a whisper but the hint of steel beneath the words told Savannah that she believed it. "I've been living a lie. I'm not who people think I am.

I don't deserve a man like Jeb." She closed her eyes. "I don't deserve *any* of this."

"Sadie, that's not true. Didn't you tell me that God brought you to Grasslands for a reason?"

"Yes, but not *this* one." Sadie lurched to her feet. "I have to go. Do you mind handling the rest of the dinner preparations without me?"

"Not at all, but—" Savannah didn't have an opportunity to finish the sentence. Sadie was already running toward the parking lot and something told Savannah to let her go this time.

God, I have no idea what's going on with Sadie, but You do. Comfort her. Remind her that You love her.

Keira was just taking a pie out of the oven when Savannah returned. "Did you find Sadie?"

All she could do was nod.

"She left."

"Left?" Maddie echoed.

Savannah wasn't sure how much to say. "Pastor Jeb asked her to go the harvest dinner tonight—as his date."

A chorus of cheers rose from the women gathered around her.

Violet grinned. "It's about time! I knew they were perfect for each other."

"Did she leave early so she could get ready?" Elise asked.

"Maybe she's going to buy a new outfit." Maddie clapped her hands together.

"I think she turned him down," Savannah told them.

Everyone stopped talking and looked at her.

"I don't believe it." Violet smacked a palm against her forehead. "It's taken Jeb months to gather the courage to ask Sadie out."

"We all know she's crazy about him, too," Elise added. "Why would she do that?"

Savannah didn't want to break a confidence, but she was concerned about Sadie. Briefly, she relayed the conversation they'd had in the prayer garden.

"Why would she think that she doesn't deserve everyone's respect? Or Jeb's attention?" Kiera asked. "Sadie is amazing. Everyone loves her."

"We've been trying to get her to see that for months," Maddie said with a sigh.

Savannah knew it wasn't simply a case of low self-esteem. The pain in Sadie's eyes had been real. Deep. She had the feeling it wasn't that Sadie didn't care about Jeb. For some reason, she didn't want him to care about *her.*

"Did she go home?"

"I'm not sure—but she asked if we could handle the dinner preparations without her."

"That doesn't sound good." Violet reached for her purse. "Sadie has poured her heart and soul into this event the last few weeks. Maybe someone should make sure she's all right."

"I'll tell the kitchen crew to keep working." Maddie disappeared through the doorway.

"I'm coming with you." Violet started after her.

"I can stay here and supervise," Savannah offered. "I know what needs to be done."

Violet cast a grateful look over her shoulder. "We'll be back in a flash."

"With Sadie," Keira added.

Savannah, remembering the tortured expression on Sadie's face, could only pray she was right.

"You're pacing."

"I'm not—" Carter stopped, midpace. "I thought you said that Savannah was going to the harvest dinner. Where is she?"

"Maddie went to the cottage to check on her a few minutes ago." Violet slipped her coat on.

"She seemed quiet when she got back this afternoon." Carter was afraid that was his fault.

"She's probably worried about Sadie." A frown creased Violet's forehead. "We all are. It isn't like her to disappear like that. Especially with the dinner this evening."

Even though Carter didn't know the church secretary very well, from the positive comments he'd heard people make about her, he had to agree.

"Savannah—" Maddie rounded the corner and came up short when she saw Carter.

"What about Savannah?" he demanded when it became clear she wasn't going to finish the sentence.

His sister glanced at Violet. "It's just girl talk."

"But she's all right?" he pressed.

"She's fine."

Carter wasn't convinced. "I need more intel."

Maddie rolled her eyes. "She's fine…physically."

Okay. Carter released the breath he'd been holding. "What else is there?"

"Do we have to spell it out for him?" Violet looked at Maddie.

"It looks that way."

"She doesn't feel attractive," Violet said.

"And she only has one dress."

"Correct me if I'm wrong, but isn't that enough? I mean, you can only wear one at a time, right?"

"It's her little black dress," Maddie said, as if that should mean something.

It didn't. "So?"

"So, Savannah doesn't think she's…little…anymore."

"She doesn't feel like it's festive enough for the dinner tonight," Violet added. "None of us can lend her anything of ours because she's in maternity clothes."

Carter locked on a single word. "Festive?"

Maddie looked up at the ceiling, as if asking for divine help. "How to explain this in a way that a guy would understand?"

Violet nibbled on her thumbnail.

"I know." She brightened. "Chrome."

"Chrome?" Maddie burst out laughing.

"Chrome," Carter repeated thoughtfully.

"Uh-huh. And…detailing."

Now he got it.

"Give me five minutes."

Savannah heard the honk of a horn in the driveway. A final boarding call that she ignored, hoping that Maddie and Violet would give up and go to the harvest dinner without her.

The knock on the door a moment later told her that they hadn't.

She pushed to her feet and drew the crocheted afghan around her shoulders like a cape. It was the only thing that fit.

"You are in a mood," Savannah muttered on her way to the door.

It swung open before she reached it and Carter stood there, his broad shoulders blocking her view of the driveway. Just the sight of him sent her heart into a freefall.

"Ready to go?"

Maddie and Violet had obviously called for reinforcements.

"I…decided to stay here tonight."

Carter's gaze lit on the afghan and then traveled down the length of her black dress before pausing to linger on her bare feet.

"Are you feeling all right?"

The genuine concern Savannah saw in his eyes made her feel better. And worse.

He was checking up on her again. Performing the duty he'd been assigned.

Frustration surged through her. She wanted Carter to let her in, to share his thoughts and hopes and fears. To seek out her company and spend time with her, not out of obligation but out of…love.

Because she'd fallen in love with *him.*

How had it happened? *When* had it happened?

And what was she supposed to do now?

"Savannah?"

Carter's husky voice filtered through her panic.

"Sorry. I'm—" *Totally in love with you.* "—just a little tired, I guess."

It was the wrong thing to say.

"Fine. We'll put in a movie."

"What?" The word came out in a squeak.

"If you're not going, neither am I."

He wasn't playing fair, Savannah thought. Carter should be with his family tonight and she didn't want to be the reason he stayed behind.

"Fine. I'll go." The words rolled out on a sigh. "I'm shaped like a pumpkin, so at least I'll blend in with the harvest decorations."

Carter's low laugh rumbled through her.

"That's right—I have something for you." He dipped his hand into his jacket pocket and pulled out a long swatch of green silk.

"It's gorgeous." Savannah touched the shimmering fabric in wonder. Maddie had probably worn it to some fancy event when she'd worked at *Texas Today*. "But I can't—" Her voice cracked as Carter tugged the yellow afghan off her shoulders and replaced it with the scarf, his large hands surprisingly gentle as he looped it around her neck.

"It matches your eyes." He nudged her toward the antique oval mirror hanging on the wall by the door. "Look."

Savannah looked. Not at the scarf or even her own reflection—but at the man standing beside her. Tall. Strong. If she took a half step backward, her head would fit perfectly in the cradle of his shoulder....

Their eyes met in the mirror.

"Did you forget what I told you a few nights ago?" he asked quietly.

Savannah hadn't forgotten anything. Not the way he'd drawn her into his arms for a slow dance. Not the kiss they'd shared.

But she remained silent, afraid that her heart would speak out of turn.

"I said you were beautiful."

"You also said the truck was pretty."

Carter grinned and glanced down, settling his hand on the curve of her waist, in the exact spot where the baby had kicked a moment ago. "Your mama can be a stubborn woman, can't she?"

Carter realized what he'd done when he saw the stunned look in Savannah's eyes.

Great. Now he was blushing like one of the teenage boys who'd been helping him fix the truck. If the guys in his unit could see him now he'd never hear the end of it.

"Don't you ever talk to the baby?" He shoved his hands in his pockets. To keep them out of trouble.

"All the time, but—"

Savannah stopped but the word hung in the air between them. Reminding Carter that he didn't have the right to touch her. To hold her.

Reminding him that she—and her baby—didn't belong to him.

Chapter Nineteen

"This was a wonderful idea." An elderly gentleman smiled at Savannah as he reached for a glass of apple cider on the buffet table. "I hope the church puts on a dinner like this next year."

"I think we—*they*—will. I already heard people talking about it," Savannah said.

"Turn on the news in the morning and you feel like crawling right back in bed. We need to take some time and remember the good things that God has done." He punctuated the statement with a decisive tap of his walking cane against the floor.

"I love the scarf," Violet whispered as she picked up an empty tray.

"It was sweet of Maddie to let me borrow it tonight."

"It's not Maddie's scarf."

"Then who does it belong to?"

Violet grinned. "Maybe someone who thinks it matches your eyes?"

It matches your eyes.

Savannah sucked in a breath.

"Carter?" She was almost afraid to believe that Violet was telling her the truth—that the scarf had been a gift from him. Or what it meant.

"We might have mentioned that you were going to skip the harvest dinner tonight because you felt a little blue. Or orange, as the case may be. We weren't sure how to convince you, so Carter took matters into his own hands."

Of course he had. Because Carter *fixed* things.

Discouragement crept in, casting a shadow over the joy that had initially blossomed in her heart.

And it explained why he hadn't spoken to her since he'd arrived at the church. He'd convinced her to attend the dinner.

"I better start washing some of these dishes." Violet darted back into the kitchen.

"Savannah?" Maddie tapped her on the shoulder. "Can you tell Elise it's time to serve the pie?"

"Sure." She wiped her hands on her apron and ducked into the kitchen. Volunteers darted back and forth but there was still no sign of Sadie.

Savannah couldn't believe she hadn't shown up.

Neither, it seemed, could Pastor Jeb. He'd poked his head in the kitchen at least a dozen times in the last hour, his worried gaze scanning the faces of the volunteers.

Elise blew a spiral of dark hair off her forehead. "I heard! We're getting the trays ready now."

Savannah walked out of the kitchen, careful not to let her gaze drift in Carter's direction. He sat at a table with some of the boys who had helped him work on the truck that afternoon. They hadn't spoken, but several times over the course of the evening Savannah had felt him watching her.

"If I could have everyone's attention for a moment, please."

Conversation instantly subsided to a hushed whisper as Pastor Jeb rose to his feet and faced the people gathered in the fellowship hall.

"I would like to thank everyone for coming to the harvest dinner this evening. I didn't plan on preaching tonight, but with Thanksgiving less than a week away, I would like to take a minute to share some of the things we can be thankful for. I receive dozens of emails and telephone calls asking for prayer, and I think it's important that we take a moment to celebrate the way God answered them."

Savannah didn't recognize many of the names and situations that Jeb talked about, but she saw people nod at each other and smile.

"The entire congregation prayed that God would provide a secretary for the church and He brought Sadie Johnson here." A long pause followed and across the room, Savannah saw Violet look at Maddie and shake her head.

The pastor's gaze shifted to the long table where Jack and Gray had assumed responsibility for Darcy and Cory while the women helped in the kitchen.

"Belle Colby is alive after an accident last summer and is in the care of gifted physicians and her loving family. Ty Garland and his daughter, Darcy, were recently reunited. Keira Wolfe recovered from a car accident and her memory has come back.... Carter Wallace is safely back with us after his tour in Afghanistan.

"I'm sure that each of you can add something of your own to this list tonight." Jeb smiled. "And if you can't think of anything, well, all you have to do is look at the people around you. Will you bow your heads and join me in prayer?"

When Savannah opened her eyes, Carter was gone.

"Do you hear that?"

Savannah glanced up from the stack of thank-you cards she'd been helping Violet address. She tipped her head. "Darcy...singing?"

"Someone sounds happy to have a few days off from school." Violet sealed an envelope and added it to the growing pile.

Violet had asked for Savannah's help writing

thank-you notes that afternoon. Belle not only received get-well cards on a regular basis, but the people in the community and surrounding area often sent flowers or small gifts to Ranchland Manor.

Everyone, Savannah thought wryly, was getting quite creative at finding things that she could do while sitting down!

"I'm hungry!" Darcy's announcement made its way to the kitchen a few seconds before she did.

"Lupita made molasses cookies. Help yourself, sweetie."

"I don't have school until next Monday." Darcy twirled her way to the plate of cookies cooling on a rack near the oven. "That means I can go riding and play with the kittens and feed the chickens every morning."

It also meant that Brian Wallace should be returning in less than forty-eight hours.

"Hi." Maddie trudged into the kitchen.

"What's wrong?" Violet, tuned in to her twin's mood, half rose to her feet.

"Pastor Jeb left another message on my voice mail."

Violet lowered her voice a notch. "Sadie still hasn't shown up for work?"

"No, and I drove by her house after I picked up Darcy from school. The lights were on, so I'm guessing that she's there, but she won't come to the door or answer the phone."

"I know that Gray suggested we give Sadie some space, but I'm worried about her," Violet murmured. "She hasn't left her house since the harvest dinner."

"That was four days ago." Maddie sank into a chair across the table from Savannah and set the mail down. "You two look busy."

"I got behind on the thank-you notes."

"That reminds me…" Maddie turned to Darcy. "What did you do with the mail, sweetheart?"

"It's in my backpack." Darcy wiggled out of the straps and handed it to Maddie.

"This one is for you, Savannah."

"Me?" Savannah glanced at the return address on the plain manila envelope and felt her heart drop to her toes. Something must have shown on her face because Maddie and Violet were at her side in an instant.

"Take a breath," Violet commanded. "Who is it from?"

Savannah pressed a hand against her stomach but that didn't stop it from churning.

"I'll be back in a few minutes."

"Are you sure?" Maddie's forehead creased. "You don't have a speck of color in your face, Savannah. Maybe you should stay here—"

"I'll be fine," Savannah whispered. She moved

toward the door on autopilot. By the time she reached the cottage, her hands were shaking so badly, she could barely tear open the envelope.

Inside the larger envelope, a handwritten note was clipped to a smaller one.

Dear Mrs. Blackmore,

This letter was discovered after your husband's personal effects were shipped back to Dallas. Please forgive the delay, but it took some time to find out where you were living.

The signature was a name Savannah didn't recognize. But she did recognize the handwriting on the outside of the smaller envelope. It was Rob's.

Dear Savannah,

If you are reading this letter, it means I finally got up enough courage to send it. I want you to know how sorry I am for leaving the way I did. It wasn't that I couldn't live with you—it was because I couldn't live with myself. I'd lied to you and destroyed your trust. I was angry with myself and with God and I didn't think I deserved a second chance with either of you.

Dozens of times, I imagined coming home to you—praying that you would forgive me.

But lately, I've started to wonder what would happen if I didn't come home. How would you know that I changed? That I recently gave my life to God? I think about you all the time and imagine what our life would look like if I had done things differently. I hope you find it in your heart to forgive me. I've made a lot of mistakes, but asking you to marry me wasn't one of them.

I hope someday I can make up for the pain I caused.

Love,

Rob.

A tear slipped down Savannah's cheek and she dashed it away with the back of her hand as the words sank in.

Everything Rob had told Carter was the way he *wanted* things to be.

She left the letter on the table and went to find him.

Maddie had said he'd been tinkering with some of the farm equipment so she veered toward the barn.

She heard Jack's low familiar drawl through the open door.

"A Lieutenant Mitchell called a little while ago. He said he's been trying to get in touch with you."

"He's been encouraging me to enlist again."

Savannah's breath tangled in her lungs and she stopped just outside the door of the barn.

"I didn't realize it was something that you've been considering. Gray and Maddie never mentioned that you planned to make the military your career."

In the short silence that followed, Savannah realized she was holding her breath.

"I'm thinking about it," Carter said slowly.

"Have you told…the rest of the family?"

"I'm not used to checking in with anyone. But no, I haven't said anything yet. I'm waiting until I know that Dad's okay."

"Ever think of staying here?"

"In Grasslands?"

If Savannah had entertained a crazy notion that Carter was as taken with the area as she was, it died a sudden death when she heard the incredulous note in his voice.

"Hey, I know it's not Fort Worth, but you have to admit, we've got a lot to offer. If a man knows what he wants," Jack added.

"And a man can do a lot of damage if he doesn't," Carter finally said.

Savannah didn't wait to hear Jack's response. It didn't matter. What mattered was that Carter didn't want a ready-made family.

He didn't want *her.*

* * *

Carter couldn't believe he was spilling his guts to Jack Colby of all people.

"You're talking about Savannah."

"She's already been hurt enough. I don't have anything to offer her and the baby."

"I guess that depends on what she wants, doesn't it?"

"I want to protect her, not cause any more pain. She's been through enough the past few months."

"Convenient, isn't it?"

"What?"

"When a guy says he wants to protect someone, he's usually protecting himself."

Carter opened his mouth to deny it—

"Don't bother. Been there, done that and I was miserable." Jack tossed the reins at him. "Here."

"You want me to put your horse away?" Carter automatically reached out and caught hold of them.

"I want you to ride him. It'll clear your head."

"There's nothing wrong with my head." It was his heart that was causing the problems.

Jack folded his arms across his chest. "You've been headed for a showdown since you got here. This is probably as good a time as any."

"A showdown?" Carter frowned. "With Savannah?"

"With God," Jack said simply. "I think it's time you stopped avoiding Him and had a long talk. I had to do the same thing a few months ago. Let go of the guilt and the anger. It's like holding on to a hot iron. The longer you do it, the more it changes you."

Carter's gut rolled over. "Guilt?"

"It's eating you up. Believe me, I recognize the symptoms." Jack met his gaze evenly. "I blamed myself for Mom's accident for months. Until Keira made me see things differently. Go on now. I have a feeling that you and God have a lot to get straightened out."

Tiger nickered and Carter scowled at the animal. "You're only on his side because he's the one who gives you oats."

"He also knows I'm right."

Carter set his heel in the stirrup and swung over the stallion's broad back.

"You've got a home here at the Colby Ranch if you want one. As far as I'm concerned, we're family."

Carter's throat tightened and he nodded curtly.

"Come on, Tiger. Let's go for a ride."

The ranch was a speck in the distance when Tiger finally downshifted from a canter to a slow walk, but it wasn't as easy for Carter.

He'd been tied up in knots since he'd returned to Texas.

If he were completely honest with himself, he knew it went farther back than a few weeks. He'd been angry with God…as long as he'd been angry with his father. It had burned deep, like that branding iron Jack had mentioned. Maybe it had already changed him.

I'm sorry, Lord. Sorry for trying to do all this on my own. For not seeking Your will and listening to Your voice. I have no idea what's going to happen in the future, but I know You're with me. I want to stick to Your path now.

And he wanted Savannah by his side.

Carter patted the horse's neck and tugged on the reins, feeling as if a weight had been lifted from his shoulders.

"Come on, Tiger, it's time to go home."

As he bent down to unlatch the gate, he saw Maddie standing by the corral, jumping up and down and waving both arms.

He waved back and loosened the reins, permission for Tiger to break into a canter as they reached the barn.

But one look at his sister's face chilled his blood.

"What's wrong?"

"You have to come to Grasslands Medical with me," Maddie choked out.

"Is Belle all right?" Carter gently took hold of her hands. "Did something happen?"

"It's not Mom." Tears filled Maddie's eyes. "It's Savannah."

Chapter Twenty

"What happened?"

Concern distilled to fear, causing Carter's blood to pump sluggishly through his veins. He was already unbuckling the girth but couldn't get his fingers to work properly.

Ty emerged from one of the outbuildings. "Go on, Carter. I'll take care of him."

Maddie struggled to match Carter's pace as he strode toward the car. "Savannah got a letter in the mail. Violet and I could tell she was upset, but she took it back to the cottage to read. I got worried when she didn't come back and went to check on her.

"She was lying on the sofa and at first I thought she was taking a nap, but she'd fainted or something. Jack and Violet drove her to the clinic to get checked out, but I thought you'd want to be with her."

"What was she doing today?" Gravel sprayed up from the tires as Carter put the truck in gear.

"Helping Violet. Savannah's been kind of quiet the past few days, but we just figured she had a lot on her mind."

Guilt burned its way through Carter. He should have bared his soul to her sooner.

When a guy says he wants to protect someone, he's usually protecting himself, Jack had said.

That's exactly what he'd been doing. He'd tried to convince himself that Savannah wouldn't be able to forgive him if she knew he hadn't been able to save Rob. That he had nothing to offer her…

"We love her, too, you know." Maddie's voice intruded on his thoughts. "She belongs here."

She belonged with him.

Carter nodded, unable to trust his voice.

The short trip into Grasslands seemed to take forever.

"Turn at the next stop sign," Maddie said.

Carter couldn't see anything that remotely resembled a hospital. When they arrived at the clinic, Carter turned to Maddie in disbelief.

"Jack brought her here?"

The clinic didn't resemble the ones he was used to seeing in the city. It looked like someone's home. But sure enough, a sign that said Grasslands Medical Clinic sprouted from the lawn.

"Don't let the outside fool you," Maddie said

briskly. "Dr. Garth knows his stuff. He can treat everything from a bee sting to a fractured bone."

The receptionist looked a little surprised when they charged through the front door into the tiny waiting room.

"We're here to see Savannah Blackmore," Carter said without preamble. "My brother Jack brought her in about half an hour ago. Where is she? Is she all right?"

The receptionist frowned. "Under law, I can't release information about a patient. Are you immediate family?"

Carter sensed that the answer to the question would determine what happened next. He glanced at Maddie.

"Close friends," she said firmly. "Savannah lives with us."

"I'll check with Nurse Hamm." The receptionist slid the glass door shut and punched a number on her phone. A moment later, she turned back to Carter and Maddie. "The nurse is with another patient at the moment. You can take a seat in the waiting room."

Carter didn't budge.

"I want to see the doctor."

"He's also with another patient at the moment—"

"Another patient," Carter interrupted. "Shouldn't he be with Savannah?"

The receptionist gave him a patient look. "I believe they're waiting for some test results at the moment."

"Come on." Maddie tugged on his arm. "I'm sure it won't be long."

Sixty seconds would be too long, but Carter let her drag him to a chair in the waiting room.

"Do you want a cup of coffee?"

"I want you to cause a disturbance while I find Savannah's room."

In spite of her concern for Savannah, Maddie grinned. "I think *you're* the one causing a disturbance," she whispered. "Do you want to see Savannah or get arrested?"

"No one will arrest me." Carter crossed his arms. "Gray won't let them."

Maddie intercepted Jack as he strode into the room with Keira at his side.

"What did the doctor say?"

"They took Savannah away the minute we got here and no one will tell me anything." Jack raked a hand through his hair. "Clinic policy, I guess."

"That's what they told us, too. Family only."

"I'm open to suggestions," Carter said.

Violet and Maddie exchanged a smile and for the first time, it didn't strike fear in Carter's heart.

"Okay, what have you got?"

* * *

Savannah moved restlessly.

Someone should turn off the timer on the oven. It kept beeping....

She opened her eyes and blinked up at the fluorescent light fixture on the ceiling.

Where was she?

The sheets hissed as she struggled to sit up.

"Hey, take it easy."

Carter?

He loomed above her. Stubble shadowed his lower jaw and there were shadows under his eyes.

"You look terrible," Savannah said without thinking. "Are you all right?"

"Am I all right?" Carter tossed the words back. "I'm fine. But you sure gave us a scare."

Savannah pressed a palm against her stomach as the fog parted. The last thing she remembered was stumbling back to the cottage, feeling lightheaded. "The baby—"

"Is doing fine." Carter pulled the chair closer to her bedside. "The doctor said that your blood pressure dropped and you had a dizzy spell. Maddie went to check on you and found you unconscious. Don't you remember?"

Savannah remembered reading Rob's letter.

And the conversation she'd overheard between Carter and Jack.

She looked away as a nurse came into the room.

"I'm Nurse Hamm. And you gave everyone quite a scare, young lady." She clucked her tongue. "Especially your fiancé."

Her fiancé?

Savannah looked at Carter and saw a red stain creep up his neck. She waited while Nurse Hamm took her vitals. When the woman bustled out of the room, she shot Carter a questioning look.

"It was Maddie and Violet's idea," Carter said gruffly. "Doctor Garth would only discuss your condition with a family member."

"Or a fiancé."

Carter nodded.

Savannah drew in a shaky breath. "And you picked the short straw?"

Her weak attempt at humor fell short at the expression on Carter's face. "Savannah—"

A rap on the door cut off the rest of what he'd been about to say. Doc Garth, a prematurely graying gentleman in jeans and cowboy boots, who looked as if he'd be more at home with a lariat in his hands than a stethoscope, ambled in. If the man hadn't been wearing a lab coat over his plaid, Western-style shirt, Savannah would have mistaken him for one of the cowboys that worked the Colby Ranch.

"How are you feeling, my dear?"

"A little better."

The doctor's eyes twinkled. "I'm glad to hear

that, but I was asking your fiancé. He looked so pale a little while ago that Nurse Hamm considered assigning him his own room."

Savannah knew better than to take the man's words seriously. Carter was a soldier. Accustomed to remaining calm in stressful situations.

Dr. Garth flipped through the sheets of paper attached to his clipboard. "I spoke with Dr. Yardley, your primary physician, a few minutes ago. She said you're scheduled for an appointment on Monday and she wants to set up an ultrasound. A standard precaution, given the fact that it appears you had some trouble a few weeks ago. Have you been getting the rest she prescribed?"

"No, she hasn't," Carter butted in.

Savannah glared at him. "I get plenty of rest." When she wasn't thinking about Carter…

The doc looked back and forth between them and his lips twitched. "Your color seems to be coming back. That's a good sign."

"Does that mean I'm free to leave now?"

"I don't see why not." Doctor Garth scratched his signature on a piece of paper. "The nurse will be back in a few minutes to give you some instructions. And—" he leveled a finger at her "—I expect you to follow them."

"I will."

"If you're planning to stay in Grasslands, I'd like to see you in a week."

Savannah didn't look at Carter, afraid that he would see the answer in her eyes.

That was one appointment she didn't plan on keeping.

Chapter Twenty-One

Preparations for the family's Thanksgiving dinner were well under way when Carter wandered into the kitchen the following morning.

Maddie and Violet sat at the counter peeling apples while Elise, who'd arrived with Cory the evening before, was rolling out dough for a piecrust. Keira was at the table, chopping up celery and onions for the stuffing.

The room was filled with women. But none of them were the one Carter had been hoping to see.

Violet spotted him in the doorway and grinned. "Looking for someone in particular?"

He had been, but there was no way he was going to admit it. He wrestled down his frustration.

After Dr. Garth had signed the necessary paperwork and released Savannah the day before, Violet and Maddie had taken charge, clucking over her like hens with a brand-new chick.

When Maddie had finally returned to the main house, she'd pulled Carter aside and handed him an envelope.

"Savannah asked me to give this to you," Maddie had said.

Carter recognized Rob's handwriting immediately.

"If you need us, we're here, you know."

Carter had hugged his sister. "I know."

He'd gone into Belle's office and shut the door, almost afraid to read the contents of the letter that had upset Savannah.

But she'd asked Maddie to give it to him.

As Carter skimmed through the words, he understood why. Rob had asked for Savannah's forgiveness because he hadn't trusted her with the truth about his feelings.

Carter was determined not to make the same mistake.

"Hi, Uncle Carter!" Darcy ambled into the kitchen, one of the kittens nestled in the crook of her arm. She made a beeline for the cookie jar.

"I don't know, squirt." Carter shook his head. "Maddie used to scold me about eating cookies right before lunch."

Darcy stood on her tiptoes and reached into the jar. "They're not for me. I told Savannah I'd bring her some."

"You saw Savannah?"

The little girl nodded. "But I wasn't disturbing her. Promise."

Carter tried to keep a straight face. "I'm sure you weren't. Savannah likes your company and it's sweet of you to bring her some cookies. She likes those, too."

"Lupita says she's eating for two an' I don't want her to get hungry on the way home." Darcy carefully deposited several oatmeal raisin cookies in a plastic bag.

Home?

Carter's stomach clenched. "What do you mean?"

"Savannah said she hasta go back to Dallas. That's where she lives."

Everyone in the kitchen had stopped working and was staring at Darcy now.

"Did Savannah tell you that she was leaving?" Maddie shot him a quick look.

"No," Carter said tightly.

But then, he hadn't given her the opportunity. He'd planned to let Savannah rest a few more hours before showing up at her door to deliver the speech he'd been rehearsing all morning.

But if Darcy was right and Savannah *was* planning to leave, it was time to take action instead.

Carter squatted down until he and Darcy were eye to eye. "How about I deliver those cookies to Savannah?"

"You want to say goodbye before she goes home, too?"

"Nope." Carter winked at her. "I want to convince Savannah that she already *is* home."

Savannah zipped the suitcase shut and looked around the room to see if she'd forgotten anything.

The cottage felt so…empty.

But it was time to make a gracious exit. Release Carter from the promise he'd made to Rob once and for all. He needed to be with his family now—not distracted by her problems.

So why did it feel as if she were going to leave a huge chunk of her heart behind when she left?

Savannah shrugged on her jacket and grabbed the suitcase, careful not to let her gaze linger on the bouquet of yellow roses the florist had delivered to her door shortly after breakfast.

Carter's thoughtful gesture had only affirmed Savannah's decision.

Maybe it was cowardly of her to leave a note instead of saying goodbye, but she couldn't run the risk that he would see the truth in her eyes. She didn't *want* to leave.

But Savannah didn't want him to feel obligated to convince her to stay, either.

She left the key on the table and blinked back the tears that threatened to spill over as she pulled the door shut behind her.

"Going somewhere?"

Savannah's heart missed a beat when she saw Carter leaning against the side of her car.

"Dallas. I have an appointment with my doctor.… What's that?" Savannah was distracted as the sunlight glinted off the object Carter casually tossed into the air and caught again.

"A spark plug."

"I thought you got the truck running."

"I did." Carter looked smug. "This is *your* spark plug."

"My—" Savannah's mouth dropped open. "But my car won't run without that. Will it?" she added.

"No, ma'am."

Carter's lazy drawl—and his equally lazy smile—threatened to sever the last thread of her composure.

"You have to put it back. Right now." Her voice shook. "I have an appointment with Dr. Yardley—"

"Next week."

He wasn't making this any easier. "And I need to find a place to live."

"Why?"

The simple question lodged in her heart. "Tomorrow is Thanksgiving. You need to focus on your family." And she was a distraction that Carter didn't need right now. "Your dad—"

"Would love to meet you," Carter interrupted.

"Everyone is expecting you to stay for Thanksgiving dinner. Why don't you stick around for a few days?"

Because it was getting harder and harder to keep her feelings to herself. Not that she could tell Carter that. If he knew how she felt about him, it would only be one more duty tying him down. Holding him back from the future God had planned for him.

"I can't," she stammered.

"Can't? Or won't?"

Savannah stiffened when Carter closed the distance between them.

"Why are you really leaving, sweetheart?"

The soft endearment broke through what was left of her defenses and the truth spilled out before Savannah could stop it.

"Because I don't want to be someone that you feel sorry for. The woman who always needs you to rescue her."

Carter didn't seem to hear her.

"I don't feel sorry for you, Savannah." He hooked a strand of hair behind her ear with a tenderness that made her heart ache. "And I *want* you to stay."

The suitcase hit the ground with a thud.

"Why?"

If Carter hadn't realized how serious the question was, he would have smiled.

"Because *you* rescued *me,*" he whispered.

"I don't understand.... I overheard you talking to Jack yesterday." Savannah's cheeks turned pink. "I didn't mean to eavesdrop. I was waiting outside the door for a chance to tell you about the letter I got...from Rob. You said you were thinking about enlisting again. That you didn't know what you...wanted."

Carter sifted through the conversation and tried not to wince.

"You should have stuck around a little longer. You would have heard the rest of the conversation."

"The rest of the conversation?"

"What you overheard...it was never about what I wanted, it was about what I thought *you* needed," Carter said quietly. "I told Jack that you've been through enough the past few months and I didn't want to cause you any more pain.

"I tried to convince myself that you and the baby deserved more than I could offer. That the best thing I could do was stand in the background and keep an eye on you. But the truth is, I'd rather be at your side." He swallowed hard. "I might not know what's going to happen down the road, but I trust that God does. He and I had a long talk and I realized something. The promise I made to Rob didn't bring us together, God did."

Tears shimmered in Savannah's eyes but there

was something else there, too. Something that gave Carter the courage to continue.

"I love you, Savannah. That's why I want you to stay."

Carter *loved* her?

Maybe, Savannah thought, she should pinch herself to see if this was real. Or maybe…

She reached out and traced Carter's angular jaw with her fingertips instead. She heard him catch his breath as he drew her into the circle of his arms.

It felt like coming home.

"I love you, too," she murmured. "But I never dreamed—" Her throat swelled shut, making it impossible to continue.

"I think both of us have been afraid to do that." Carter's arms tightened around her. "But you can trust me, Savannah. With today…and whatever happens tomorrow."

Tomorrow suddenly looked a whole lot brighter.

Carter's expression turned serious. "There is one thing we have to talk about, though."

Savannah's heart dipped. "All right."

"You have to let me teach Hope how to throw a football and change a flat tire." Mischief sparked in Carter's eyes.

She couldn't believe that God had brought this amazing man into her life.

"What if she wants to take ballet?" Savannah teased, responding in kind.

"Then I'll be sitting in the bleachers, right next to her beautiful mother, with a bouquet of roses."

Savannah felt as if her heart were going to burst. "Agreed," she whispered.

Carter bent his head and his lips captured hers. When the kiss ended, Savannah could feel her heart racing in time with his.

"So I have a question," Carter murmured in her ear.

"I believe you only get one," Savannah said promptly.

"Will you go out with me?" Carter looked down at her, his smile a little unsteady. "On a real date?"

"That sounds…wonderful."

"I was thinking…dinner."

"When and where?"

"Tomorrow? Turkey with all the trimmings." Carter pointed to the main house. "Right over there."

"With your family?"

"Yes." Carter tipped his head. "Is that all right?"

"All right?" Savannah closed her eyes and felt the steady drum of Carter's heart against her cheek. "It sounds absolutely perfect to me."

Chapter Twenty-Two

"You were up early this morning."

Carter looked up and saw Maddie in the doorway, a cup of coffee in one hand.

"So are you."

"I had a hard time sleeping last night," she admitted. "Did you convince Savannah to spend Thanksgiving with us?"

Carter had a hard time keeping a smile from surfacing. "I think so. She'll be here in a few minutes."

"Good." Maddie released a heartfelt sigh. "We don't want any extra chairs at the table today."

She was still holding out hope their father would return.

They all were.

But now, Carter realized it was more important to see his dad's face again than to hear his explanations.

Lord, bring him back safely and we'll go from there.

Moving forward with God's help. Just the way Gray had said.

"Come on, you two." Violet shooed them toward the dining room. "We've got a lot of last-minute things to do."

Things that kept him and Savannah apart.

Carter wanted to be alone with her, but decided he was willing to share her with his family for a few hours.

"Dinner is served!" Maddie called out.

Landon Derringer carried the turkey into the dining room and Violet lit two slim taper candles in the centerpiece.

Jack waited until everyone found a seat at the table.

"Mom started a tradition when Violet and I were young. On Thanksgiving, she would choose a portion of scripture, reminding us how much we have to be thankful for. I took the liberty of carrying on the tradition this year."

Under the table, Carter felt Savannah squeeze his hand.

"'We ought always to thank God for you, brothers, and rightly so, because your faith is growing more and more, and the love every one of you has for each other is increasing.'"

Jack cleared his throat. "I think that's been happening the past five months. Our faith has grown—and so has our love for each other. Mom would say we have a lot to be thankful for today."

A murmured chorus of heartfelt *amens* followed.

"Amen," Cory chimed in. "Can we eat now?"

Gray laughed as Elise tried to shush her son. "We sure can."

Jack began to carve the turkey as the side dishes made their way around the table.

Above the hum of conversation, a car door slammed.

Maddie jumped to her feet and ran to the window, her lips forming a single word.

Dad.

A collective sigh circled the table as Maddie shook her head.

Savannah realized how desperately everyone wanted Brian Wallace to show up. To keep the promise he'd made to his family.

"Can I have another roll, Savannah?" Darcy pointed to the basket. "Before Uncle Carter eats them all?"

The comment brought a smile to everyone's face and broke through the shadow of silence that had fallen.

"Here you go." Savannah made a point to hold

it out of Carter's reach as she passed it to the little girl.

Maddie smiled at her. "I'm glad that Carter talked you into staying, Savannah."

"They're gettin' married," Darcy said matter-of-factly.

Heads swiveled in their direction.

Savannah felt her cheeks begin to glow and she looked helplessly at Carter. "We aren't—"

"What makes you say that, Darcy?" Violet interrupted.

"I saw them kissing yesterday. Can I have some mashed potatoes, please?"

No one, Savannah noted, passed the mashed potatoes. She wanted to slide under the table—except that she wouldn't fit.

"If you marry Savannah, she'll be my aunt, won't she, Uncle Carter?" Darcy had obviously thought this through.

"And mine, right?" Cory wasn't going to be left out.

"That's right." Carter winked at her.

"Oh, don't blush, Savannah." Keira nudged her shoulder. "This family is getting so big, you may as well enjoy the attention while you can."

Carter took pity on her and cleared his throat. "Right now, I think the *turkey* needs some attention."

"Fine—but don't think you're off the hook,

little brother," Maddie said. "We expect you to keep us in the loop."

"Whatever you say, sis," Carter muttered under his breath.

Savannah smiled despite herself.

"Not quite what you imagined when you prayed for a family, is it?" Carter murmured in her ear a few moments later.

"No," Savannah whispered back. "It's much, much better."

No one seemed in a hurry to leave the table, lingering over dessert.

Waiting.

Carter caught hold of Savannah's hand underneath the table.

"Would you like to go for a walk?"

There was a look in his eyes that made Savannah's heart skip a beat.

She nodded. "I'll help clear the table first."

"Oh, no, you won't," Violet said cheerfully. "We already assigned a cleanup crew and your name isn't on it."

Maddie made a shooing motion with her hand. "Go on. I'm sure you've got a lot to talk about. After we take care of the dishes, we're going to drive into Grasslands and visit Belle."

Savannah gave Carter a questioning look. She knew his feelings toward Violet and Jack had changed, but she wasn't sure how he felt about Belle.

"Do you mind if we delay our walk for a few hours?"

"I was thinking the same thing."

His smile took her breath away and he turned to Maddie.

"We'll come with you."

Carter followed Gray's car as it turned into the parking lot at Ranchland Manor.

The last time he'd been here, he'd heard Belle Colby say his father's name.

Savannah laid her hand on his arm. "We don't have to go inside."

"Yes, we do." Another step forward, with God's help.

Gray would be amazed to know Carter was following his advice.

The young woman at the reception desk, who looked barely out of her teens, greeted them with a bright smile. Her badge was the kind with the adhesive back and the name Taylor, embellished with several curlicues, had been neatly printed in blue marker.

"Can I help you?"

"Must be new here," Maddie murmured.

"I just started yesterday," came the cheerful response. "So far, it's going really well."

"I'm glad to hear that." Violet ducked her head to hide a smile. "We're here to see Belle Colby."

"Colby— *Oh*." The girl's gaze swept over them and she lowered her voice a respectful notch. "You're Mrs. Colby's family?"

"That's right." Gray didn't miss a beat.

For the first time, Carter didn't feel any resentment that Gray considered Belle family.

"She's our most popular patient today."

Jack frowned. "Popular?"

The aide nodded. "She's already had a visitor today."

"Who was it?" Gray demanded. "A woman or a man?"

Taylor bit her lip. "Did I do something wrong?" she stammered. "I didn't see a note that she couldn't have visitors."

"You didn't do anything wrong," Maddie intervened, her smile meant to temper Gray's curt response. "It's just that we're not sure who it could have been, because everyone is…here."

"Not everyone," Jack muttered.

Carter looked at Gray. His dad knew where they were and what had happened to Belle. Was it possible he would have stopped by the convalescent home to see her first?

"Let me see." Taylor checked the sign-in sheet. "I must have been on the phone at the time. She signed in a little after ten…. I can't read the signature."

She.

Carter released the breath he hadn't realized he'd been holding.

"Can I see it?" Gray sounded more in control now but Taylor still looked nervous as she handed him the clipboard.

"I can't make out the name, either." He frowned. "You said it was a woman? What did she look like?"

Taylor took a step back.

"Cop voice," Elise whispered.

"Sorry...Taylor." Gray flashed an apologetic smile. "Habit."

Taylor tipped her head. "She was short. Thin. Glasses."

"That sounds like Sadie," Savannah ventured.

"You know what a sweetheart she is," Violet said. "She was probably visiting some of the residents who don't have family and stopped in to see Mom."

Jack took Keira's hand. "Makes sense."

But it didn't erase the look of disappointment on the faces of the people gathered around the desk. Carter felt Savannah rest her head on his shoulder. Being on the receiving end of comfort was a new experience. One it would take some time to get used to.

A lifetime, if he was lucky.

Violet was peering at the clipboard. "I've seen

Sadie's handwriting. It doesn't look anything like this."

"Maybe she was in a hurry," Maddie said.

"Maybe, but—"

"I was hoping to see you before my shift ended." A dark-haired nurse in lime-green scrubs and a colorful bandana emerged from the backroom.

Taylor retreated quickly. No doubt relieved to hand them over to someone else, Carter thought wryly.

"How is Mom doing?" Jack asked.

The nurse hesitated. "Belle seemed a little restless this morning," she admitted. "There've been a lot of people in and out of our facility visiting family over the past few days, so it's possible she's reacting to subtle changes in the environment. I made a note for the doctor to check on her tomorrow when he comes in, but I'm sure there's nothing to worry about."

Then why did she looked worried?

One glance at his siblings told Carter they had the same thought.

"We put out coffee and refreshments in the lounge for family members today in honor of Thanksgiving." The phone rang and the nurse reached for it. "Please help yourself."

The aroma of cinnamon scented the air as everyone made their way to Belle's room at the end of the hall. They could hear murmured conversations and laughter behind the doors.

"It's too gloomy in here." Maddie strode to the window and pulled open the drapes, flooding the room with afternoon sunlight.

"Someone fixed Mom's hair." Violet was staring down at her mother. "Do you think it was Sadie?"

Belle's thick copper hair lay in a neat braid over one shoulder. A vase of bright yellow daisies trimmed with delicate baby's breath graced the nightstand.

Jack bent down and kissed his mother on the forehead. "Hey, Mom. It's Jack. Keira and I stopped by to say hello."

"I'm here, Mom." Violet nudged her brother to the side and took Belle's hand. "Maddie and Ty and Gray and Carter are here, too."

Carter didn't feel awkward being included anymore. It felt…right.

"When you wake up, you're going to have a lot of weddings to help plan. Me and Landon are first, by the way." Violet cast a teasing glance at Maddie.

Belle's head rolled to the side and a soft moan escaped her lips.

"She seems different today," Violet murmured. "Do you think she's in pain?"

Carter put his arm around Violet's slender shoulders. "The nurse said it was normal, remember?"

She leaned against him. "That's right."

"I think we should pray for her." Jack took hold of Maddie's hand. She, in turn, took hold of Savannah's until the entire family was linked together in a circle around Belle's hospital bed.

"Lord, thank You for bringing us together. We can see that You are at work in our lives. We see Your hand in the things that have happened the past few months and because You love us, we trust You with the future. You've blessed us with so much—how can we doubt Your love?"

Carter didn't. Not anymore. Not in a million years would he have imagined that God would bring a woman like Savannah into his life.

Thank You, Father. I'm going to be the kind of husband Savannah deserves, and I'm going to raise Hope as if she were my own.

"We—" Jack's voice faltered. "Mom?"

Carter heard Savannah gasp and his eyes flew open. Maddie pressed her hand against her lips.

"What—" A second later, he understood why.

Belle's breathing had changed. The sudden silence more frightening than the soft moans they'd gotten used to hearing.

Gray turned to Elise. "Call the nurse, sweetheart," he said in a hoarse whisper.

"No." Jack's throat convulsed. "Wait."

"What's happening?" Maddie stared down at

Belle, her eyes dark with rising panic. "What's wrong with her?"

"Mom?" Jack's hands closed around the metal rail, his gaze riveted on Belle's face. "I think she's…waking up."

Maddie let out a strangled cry and Carter took a step closer to the bed.

Velvet brown eyes blinked at the faces above her.

Maddie and Violet clung to each other, unable to believe that after all these months, Belle was with them again.

"Thank You, God."

Carter wasn't sure who said the words, Gray or Jack, but it didn't matter.

He looked down at Savannah. Tears streamed down her face but she was smiling.

"Carter—"

"I know." He pulled Savannah into his arms.

No matter what happened next, they did have a lot to be thankful for.

* * * * *

Dear Reader,

Some of my favorite books (to read *and* write) are centered around a holiday, so it was a double blessing to be asked to participate in the Texas Twins continuity and have Thanksgiving play a significant role in the story.

While writing Savannah and Carter's story, I was challenged and encouraged to count the blessings in my own life. Sometimes when we experience trials, it's easy to forget just how much there is to be thankful for. Maybe we should all take Savannah's advice and "count to ten" on a regular basis!

I hope you've enjoyed the series so far. Faith. Friendship. Family…and secrets. What could be more exciting?

You won't want to miss *Reunited for the Holidays* by Jillian Hart, book six in the Texas Twins series.

Keep smiling and seeking Him!

Questions for Discussion

1. Have you ever made a promise to a friend? What was it? Did you find it easy or difficult to keep?

2. Do you think Carter's siblings, Maddie and Gray, did the right thing when they waited for him to return from Afghanistan before they told him what had happened in the family? Why or why not?

3. Brian Wallace and Belle Colby kept a secret from their children. Do you think it's ever all right to withhold the truth about something from a family member? In what kinds of situations might it be justified?

4. Both Savannah and Carter had experienced loss, but they handled it in different ways. What were they? Which character could you identify with more?

5. In what ways did the hero and heroine's life experiences impact their faith in a positive way? A negative way?

6. Savannah assumed that Carter was only helping her out of a sense of duty or obligation.

Have you ever misunderstood someone's intentions? What was the situation? What was the outcome?

7. What was the turning point in Carter and Savannah's relationship?
8. Can you think of ten things, right now, that the Lord has blessed you with? What are they?
9. Discuss some of the challenges that soldiers might face when they return home from active duty. Which one do you think Carter struggled with the most? Give specific examples from the book to support your answer.
10. How did Carter and Savannah use their talents to serve the church? How have you used your unique gifts and talents in your local community or congregation?
11. Brian Wallace loved his children, but he was an absentee father while they were growing up. Share your views on "quality versus quantity" as it relates to parenting.
12. Carter and his siblings spent a lot of time waiting. For Brian to return and for Belle to show signs of improvement after her accident. Have

you ever experienced a "season" of waiting? Describe. Did it strengthen or weaken your faith?

13. What was your favorite scene in the book?

14. Sadie Johnson tells Savannah that she doesn't "deserve" Pastor Jeb's attention—or his affection. What would you tell a friend who feels the same way?

15. Pastor Jeb quotes a verse from the Psalms during his message one Sunday morning. Have there been times you felt that God was "carrying" you? Describe the situation.